THEIR RECKLESS BRIDE

BRIDGEWATER MÉNAGE SERIES - BOOK 11

VANESSA VALE

Copyright © 2019 by Vanessa Vale

This is a work of fiction. Names, characters, places and incidents are the products of the author's imagination and used fictitiously. Any resemblance to actual persons, living or dead, businesses, companies, events or locales is entirely coincidental.

All rights reserved.

No part of this book may be reproduced in any form or by any electronic or mechanical means, including information storage and retrieval systems, without written permission from the author, except for the use of brief quotations in a book review.

Cover design: Bridger Media

Cover photos: Period Images; Deposit Photos: Krivosheevv

1

 RACE

"You're on the wrong side of the law, Sheriff." Father's voice carried to where I was positioned, hidden thirty feet above on the bluff. His voice was rough and deep, full of evil intent as it echoed off the rock. His clothes were old and tattered in spots. He was filthy, the hot sun making rivulets of sweat slide through the dust on his neck.

"Wrong side of a gun," Travis replied, standing beside him and laughing, then spitting a huge wad of chewing tobacco onto the dirt at his feet. I didn't have to be close to him to know he smelled to high heaven. Even if the creek behind the house had been flowing instead of all but dried up this time of the year, it wouldn't matter. This man simply refused to bathe.

Father laughed, confident that while they'd been chased by a two-man posse, he and my brother were the ones who were waving their weapons. It was as if they were on the right side of the law and not part of the infamous Grove gang who'd just robbed the bank in Simms.

I slithered closer to the edge of the bluff, the tall grass shielding me from sight. Below was the bend in the creek and where Father and Travis had hidden in the grove of cottonwood trees that lined the bank, waiting for the sheriff to catch up, then ambush.

The two lawmen had been forced to dismount and now their horses were drinking from the water, unaware their riders' lives were being threatened.

"Should we kill them, Travis, or perhaps shoot 'em and leave 'em for the buzzards?"

Father would. He was a mean, cruel man who'd shoot a man and leave him to suffer a slow death, bleeding out and dying alone in the middle of nowhere.

It would be a shame though. The men who stood with their hands raised, their weapons tossed on the ground at their feet, were fine specimens worthy of life. Worthy of taking my time to study, and not after Father put bullets in their bellies.

From my vantage, I could easily discern the tin star on the sheriff's broad chest. His hat shielded his eyes from the sun, so I couldn't tell what color they were, but he had dark hair that curled from beneath the hat. His mouth formed a thin line, his square jaw clenched tight. He wasn't happy. Despite being hidden by his snug shirt and trim pants, every muscle in his body was taut. His hands were by his sides, his long fingers flexing and curling. It was as if he were tightly coiled, awaiting the moment when he could strike. If he weren't being held at gunpoint, his size and weight would make him a formidable opponent. I wasn't short, quite tall for a woman, but I estimated I'd come up to his nose, at most. My father and brother were short of stature and lean, making their weapons the only leveler of this showdown.

Looking at the sheriff stirred something in me. Awakened it. Made me see a man with different eyes, those of a woman interested in a man. Attracted to one. Why him? Why now? I'd never felt any kind of stirring of desire before this moment. My heart had never skipped a beat, my breath never catching from just a glimpse. While I was most definitely a woman—my tightly bound breasts were proof of that—I'd never behaved as one. Not with being raised as the only female in the family. I never imagined I'd ever be like one... wearing comely dresses, corsets, pretty sun bonnets, let alone wanting a man.

Every one I'd come across had been mean, ornery and ugly.

Was this sudden keen interest the reason for why I found the man standing beside him equally appealing? I'd never set eyes upon a man with red hair before. He wasn't wearing a hat, so the dark auburn locks curled and fell over his forehead in a rakish manner. Even from the distance between us, I couldn't miss his green eyes, the same color as the grass I laid upon. He didn't look afraid or panicked. He looked... livid. His anger toward my father and brother was obvious.

I crawled a little closer to the edge, the soft grass a cushion beneath me, pulled my gun up beside me. Ogled. Perhaps because I was used to Father's threats and menace, I remained calm in such a dire situation and studied the handsome duo. Oh my. They were virile. Intense. Imposing, even staring down the barrel of a gun.

Father and Travis felt like men when they were waving their guns. They needed the weapons to make them powerful. The other two... they exuded it naturally.

Knowing they were chasing after some of the Grove gang, eager to bring them to justice, only added to their appeal. They weren't like my family. They were better. *More.* And that made me that much more intrigued by them. For the first time in my life, I wanted to run my hands over a man. *Two men.* I wanted to feel their hard bodies, cup their jaws with my palm and feel the rasp of their whiskers. I wanted to feel small, feminine. I wanted to *feel.* With them, I knew I would. But they wouldn't remain passive like they were now. They'd take what they wanted from me.

The idea of that was so wrong, for Father did just that. Oh, not in the same way, but he took. And took. Father— and Travis as well— made my life utterly miserable. I'd cooked and cleaned like a servant. Slave, more like it, since I was never paid for my efforts. When Father took to drink, I hid, discovering he liked to take out any anger he had on me. Travis never protected me, only told me I'd deserved it. That I was just a useless woman.

Their control over me had me constantly teetering between the right and wrong side of the law. I'd never committed any of the crimes my family name was known for, but I was definitely guilty by association. I could have gone to the sheriff at any time and turned them in, told them exactly where they could be found, when their next robbery would occur. But I hadn't, not once, because I was afraid for my life. Father wasn't a man to hug. No, he was a man who hit.

And then, he'd discovered how a mere woman could be of value. The *only* way he thought a woman could be worthy. The asshole.

That was why I was here now. The lawmen weren't the only ones seeking retribution.

"Give it up, Grove," the sheriff said. His voice was as sharp as a knife blade.

Father and Travis laughed, clearly believing they were the ones in control in this moment, that they held the power, that the lives of the two men were theirs to extinguish if they desired.

"You're not in a position to make any kind of threats, Sheriff," Travis said. "We're the ones holding the guns."

They weren't the only one. Staying low, I settled my weapon before me, aimed. I was more familiar with my rifle, but the Colt I'd taken from Barton Finch would work. Thinking back, I should have shot him with it. Stupid mistake on my part, leaving him alive after what he'd intended. I'd been so angry with Father that I'd stormed off. Tracked him and Travis down.

I'd dreamed of killing what was left of my family for a long time. Lain in bed at night and imagined how I would do it. Longed to be free of them. Father had taught my brothers how to shoot, and he'd humored me by allowing me to practice beside them, but he probably never imagined I'd aim the gun at him. And fire.

I had a hatred for them that practically festered.

I might share the same blood, might live in the same ramshackle house, but I wasn't anything like them. My dark thoughts were solely focused on them, no one else. I didn't wish anyone else harm. I wouldn't let them kill two innocent men. Not men doing their job, trying to keep the peace. Trying to mete out justice.

"Time to meet your maker, Sheriff." Father cocked his gun.

So did I. And I fired first.

The loud report made the sheriff flinch, but it was Father who fell to the ground.

"That's for giving me to Barton Finch," I whispered, watching Father writhe as he pressed his hand against the bullet hole in his thigh, the blood seeping around his fingers. He shouted out in pain, swearing, searching for where the shot had come.

I took the moment where Travis stared down at him, stunned and confused at what had just occurred to cock my gun again. It wasn't hard to aim; Travis was an unmoving target, much larger than an empty whiskey bottle I was used to. Fired.

He fell where he stood.

"And that, Travis, is for being an asshole."

The sheriff and the other man instinctively crouched to try to make themselves smaller, but went over to Father and Travis, grabbed their weapons so they were no longer a threat.

I hadn't killed them, but there was no way Father or Travis would hurt the other men now. Ending their lives would be too good for them, too easy. I shot them just as they'd have done to the sheriff and other man. But unlike my family, I'd made sure the wounds I inflicted were survivable injuries, if seen to promptly. We were a few miles from Simms. The sheriff could drag their bleeding bodies back to town to be tended to by the doctor, then hanged. Or, he could leave them to rot. It was his choice. Either way suited me just fine.

Tucking the weapons in the back of their pants, the sheriff and the other man picked up their own guns, whipping about to point them in my direction. Their gazes searched once along the edge of the bluff for the shooter. For me.

Perhaps I was as cruel as my father to leave him and Travis to suffer, but after what he'd done to me? After he *gave* me to Barton Finch this morning, I had no mercy left. I'd escaped being raped. Barely. I just hadn't expected revenge to come so quickly. Now, I had it. I stood and adjusted my hat, looked down at the scene one last time, a smile on my face seeing Father and Travis suffer and writhe. Fuck, I should have finished Barton Finch when I had the chance, then all of the Grove gang would be either dead or hanged soon enough.

When the two other men saw me, I stared at them for one brief moment and wondered what it would be like to be theirs, knowing it was never to be.

Two men didn't want one woman, and I barely behaved like one. I didn't even own a dress. My hair was long and wild, always in a braid and tucked up beneath my hat to stay out of the way. If that weren't unappealing enough, there was one thing even worse. I was a Grove.

2

Hank

"Who the fuck was that?" I said, making my way over to my horse, grabbing hold of the reins. The satchel they'd used to steal the cash was beside them on the ground and I grabbed that, tied it to the saddle bag. I didn't want anything to happen to all that hard-earned—and easily stolen— money. As for the men…

I was sweating, my heart pounding, realizing how close to death we'd come. It hadn't been the first time, and it probably wouldn't be the last. But, fuck.

The man, hell, he couldn't be more than a teenager, had taken down the Grove gang with two bullets. They'd been running wild for years, wreaking havoc, escalating their crimes to include murder. Ours were almost on that list. Except the kid had saved us, and I wanted to talk with him.

The band of thieves and murderers had killed my father,

and I'd replaced him as sheriff solely for retribution. To see those fuckers behind bars. Hanged.

And now, with one bullet, then another, two of them were done for. Only one more remained wanted. Now that I didn't have two guns pointed at me, I could relish the knowledge that they would pay. That they would feel the rough rope about their necks and know they were headed to hell. I wanted to see them behind the bars of a jail cell, but knowing they were bleeding all over the ground was enough for now. They weren't going anywhere. Not with the wounds they had. Fuck those men. I wanted that kid.

He'd stared down at us, and I'd gone still, frozen as if caught out in a blizzard in January. I'd caught the angle of his jaw, but the rest of his face was in shadow beneath the brim of his hat. His figure was slim beneath the loose shirt and pants, that of a man not grown fully. A gangly youth.

"I have no idea. Not the last member of that fucking group. Too small based on witnesses. All I know is we're not dead," Charlie replied, easing his animal away from the water, patting the animal's sleek neck, then mounting easily. I didn't have to tell him my intentions; he knew we were going after the kid.

I was completely baffled by my reaction to seeing him standing up on the bluff. My cock had hardened like a fucking fence post. Perhaps it was an instinctive reaction to almost dying... but I'd been close to death before and my dick had never risen to the occasion. Being sheriff wasn't the safest job; my father's demise was proof of that. As I thought about it, my cock stand hadn't happened *when* we were about to die, only when I stared up at our savior.

When the shot rang out, I sucked in my breath, thinking I'd taken the bullet. But it hadn't even come from Grove's gun, but from somewhere above us on the bluff. The location, with the rocky slope behind us, the land turning abruptly so one couldn't see far, as well as the thick stand of trees was perfect for an ambush. We'd been stupid to ride into it, but we hadn't been expecting to find the bank robbers this close to town. The fact that they hadn't been up on the bluff to pick us off only went to their interest in killing face to face. It seemed someone else had already claimed that spot and saved our sorry asses. Thank fuck.

"Hey! Are you going to fucking leave us here?" the elder Grove shouted, his voice now laced with pain instead of cockiness.

I held my horse's reins taut and looked down at Marcus Grove as he dripped sweat and grimaced in pain. His hand was on his thigh and blood oozed around his fingers. As for his son, he lay a few feet away, feet in the creek. He'd been shot in the gut, although blood stained his side, probably missing all the vital organs. He, too, was perspiring heavily, but he was pale, his breathing ragged. There was no chance either of them could mount their horses, wherever the fuck they were hidden. They would die out here... eventually. Perhaps this was better than waiting to be hanged. Hours of suffering.

I had little sympathy for them. My father had spent the last year of his life hunting those fuckers down. I should just shoot them dead and be done with it, taken them down like a horse with a broken leg. I wasn't sure if the kid was a bad shot or if he'd actually aimed perfectly. Had he intended on killing or just injuring them? Had he heard what Grove had intended, to leave us for the buzzards? Was this turnabout or had his intention been for them to suffer? Or eventually have them feel nooses about their necks?

Who the fuck was that kid and what had he been doing out here?

I stared down at two of the men who'd driven my every action since my father's death. Who kept me from the quiet ranch life. They were pitiful. A waste of humanity. And I was leaving them behind. Crazy, I knew, but I had more important things to deal with right now.

"Don't worry, we'll send help," I muttered, nudging my horse into motion, not looking back. God might send me to hell, but many people had suffered because of the Grove gang. I didn't really give a shit they were hurting or bleeding out and I doubted Charlie did either. I might be the sheriff and strive for justice, but seeing them taken down like rabid dogs *was* justice. My father would have shot them dead. Ironic, as that was how he was killed.

"By morning," Charlie added with a humorless grin. His money was—had been—in the Simms bank. Before he left England, he'd saved some from his military life, then added to it here, working in a copper mine in Butte, then becoming part owner. He had wealth now, something he'd told me he'd strived for his entire life. It was important to him, only in that his mind was at ease that he would never be without food or shelter. He could survive. We lived at Bridgewater, had a house big enough for the family we'd someday have. But it was our goal to add acreage, raise cattle. Work a ranch of our own. A simple life. Nothing more.

Maybe instead of shooting the Groves outright, I should've thrown them over the backs of their horses and led them to be patched up by the doc. They could be tossed in jail later since the circuit judge wouldn't show up for a few days yet. They'd be found guilty, no question. But they could just bleed all over the ground and fucking wait. I had a more important thing to do: find the kid and discover why he made my dick hard. That shit wasn't normal for me.

The groans and swearing fell away as we made our way

north along the creek bank until the bluff lowered and met the flat land. Cutting across the water, we turned in the direction the gunman must have taken. There were no trees here, nothing to obstruct our view. There was nothing in front of us but miles of open prairie. He might be nimble and quick, but he wouldn't have made it out of sight without a horse. Charlie turned and cut up along the bluff's edge to where he'd have perched and fired. Even though it was a hot day, it had been a wet summer and the grass was tall and green still. We couldn't miss the trampled path the kid had taken and we turned to follow.

"She's fast, I'll give her that," he said, riding at a quick pace alongside me, but not too hard as to tire our horses.

I tipped back my hat. "Her?" I said.

He looked to me, raised a brow. Grinned. "The woman who saved us back there."

Woman?

I sighed, more relieved than when I thought I'd been shot. "Oh, thank fuck."

He barked out a laugh. "Bloody hell, man. You thought *she* was a *he,* didn't you?"

"My cock had it right," I said, shifting in the saddle as I remembered *her* standing above us, the gun in her hand. "Have you ever met a woman who wore pants? That's not normal for a woman, even around here. Besides, we almost died. I'm allowed a little leniency."

I felt the heat of embarrassment in my cheeks. I was the sheriff. I chased bad men. Saved people, not the other way around. If I couldn't tell a man from a woman, it was possible I'd lost my balls.

"We were lucky she was there." He laughed, then scratched his chin. "I'll admit, the pants had me fooled for a moment, but it was her shape—"

"What shape?" I countered. I didn't remember the curve of womanly hips, the lush swell of a pair of breasts beneath the baggy men's clothing. And yet, I'd still gotten hard. Still was.

"Her long neck, the tip of her chin. Her lithe figure." He looked ahead, but I could tell he was envisioning her in his mind. "My little warrior."

I didn't miss his use of the word *my*.

"A woman who has the balls to shoot two men in cold blood, dresses like a man and has no discernible curves," I said. It was very uncomfortable riding a horse with a hard-on. "Why do I want to fuck the breath right out of her?"

He looked to me. "Because the second she fired that gun and saved our sorry asses, she became mine."

I took off my hat, set it in my lap, wiped my forehead with my sleeve. I offered him a dark look.

"Ours," he corrected, realizing his error.

I paused. "You don't think she's one of them, got angry at the others and decided to shoot them?"

Charlie looked off in the distance. Considered. "Not a chance. Eyewitnesses describe the third man as stocky. Tall."

I nodded. "That's what I thought as well. She's not one of them, but she definitely hates them for some reason. We already have something in common."

"She's not a meek miss, simpering over ribbons and bows," he added. "Neither of us want that in our woman. Hell, if I'd wanted that, I'd have stayed in England. This one's fierce, brave and because... fuck, I don't know, but I feel the same way. I can't wait to strip her bare and learn every inch of her."

"I've never stripped the pants off of someone before," I countered, setting my hat back on my head, nudging my horse a little faster.

She was a mystery. An enigma. I was eager to learn everything about her. Who she was. Why she was there on the bluff. Why she shot the Grove men. Why the fuck she was hiding the fact that she was a woman. Any female dressed like that was clearly keeping her gender a secret. She didn't want to be discovered, or she didn't want it to be known that she was a *she*.

"Those men's clothes were overlarge. I'd bet that bag of money she's got all kinds of curves hidden. Remember, if we can't see them, no one else can."

So true. We'd be the only men who saw what was beneath. And that made my cock even harder, knowing she'd sealed her fate. She was ours.

Whoever she was.

A tiny, one room cabin, if it could be called that, came into view in the distance. Dilapidated and leaning precipitously, a strong wind would finish it off. Set on the bank of a small creek—a different one from where we'd been ambushed—I was surprised it hadn't been washed away during a heavy spring run-off. There was nothing out here for miles but open prairie, Simms several miles away. I saw no fencing for a horse pen or even an outhouse. A beautiful but lonely spot. Surely, no one had lived there for years. Small animals, perhaps, or someone seeking shelter from a storm... or hiding.

I slowed, then we halted our horses a good distance away. We saw no woman, only a horse grazing. All was quiet except the wind.

"The path leads right to it," Charlie said, pointing from where we were and the broken grass that went directly toward the rundown structure. He dismounted, patted his horse's flank and dropped the reins to let him graze. "If we're approaching, we need to take her by surprise. No way in hell am I letting her shoot me."

I agreed with my friend. The only holes in a body I was interested in were hers. All three of them, and we'd claim each one of them soon enough.

3

 RACE

I swiped at my brow, tucked a long strand that had come loose from my braid behind my ear. My emotions were restless. Unsettled.

Instead of remembering the look of Father and Travis bleeding and writhing, nor their sounds of anger and pain at being shot, I couldn't get the *other* two men out of my mind. The rugged build of the dark-haired sheriff. The strong jaw and muscled torso of the other. *Both* of them appealed to my feminine senses and that had never happened before. I hadn't even realized I had any. Until them.

These lingering thoughts did nothing to ease the heat that had built within me, and it wasn't from the strong sun. I crouched down beside the creek's edge, letting my fingers dip in the cool water, watched as a leaf floated by, swirling and working its way downstream. I wondered where it would go, what it would be like to go with the current and see where it took me. Away from here, away from the life in which I was trapped.

While I may have shot my family—and without a bit of remorse—they were the least of my problems. Surely, the sheriff was leading them back to town now and to jail. The doctor would tend to their wounds and they'd be fine, at least until they were hanged. But Barton Finch...

I cupped my hands together, leaned down and splashed water on my face. Again, then again, as if I could ever get clean from what he'd done. What he'd intended to do.

He was still out there, and now not only evil, but ornery as hell by being bested by a mere woman, and would want revenge. I'd kneed him in the balls and he'd dropped like a stone, then curled up in a ball on the floor in his filthy house. I'd fled when he began to vomit. That hadn't been the *payment* he'd expected out of me. Once recovered, he'd go straight to the house. He'd hear soon enough of the Grove gang's capture. Instead of giving him money, Father had given Barton Finch *me*. Father had told him I was *virgin pussy to be broken in*. It wasn't a prize he'd be denied. He'd come looking for me. To claim payment.

I had no doubt. The man was more ruthless and cold-hearted than Father. I hated my family—enough to shoot them in cold blood—but I was scared of Barton Finch. I couldn't return to the cabin as it would be the first place he'd look for me once recovered. Not that I had any interest in returning to the cabin. Ever. There was nothing there for me. Nothing of sentimental value. This shack, a place I'd come to in the past when I'd needed to be alone, would be my shelter until I considered my options.

I sighed and pulled a handkerchief from my pants' pocket, wet it, then ran it over the back of my neck. Undoing a button on my shirt, I slid it over my skin above the binding on my breasts. That snug material did the job of hiding my figure, but it also made me hot and sticky. I was ready to strip and bathe in the cool water, don clean clothes I'd put in my saddle bag along with some food I'd grabbed from the house this morning, enough for a day or two.

I was safe here. It wasn't much, but there was no one around for miles.

Or so I thought.

A sound had me whipping my head about. I stood abruptly at the sight of a man. My hand went to my hip out of habit for my gun, but it wasn't there.

"Looking for this?" It was the sheriff, holding up my weapon. Barton Finch's weapon I'd taken from him. I'd set it and its holster upon a large rock.

With a finger, he tipped the brim of his hat back, cocked his head and eyed me. His casual stance made me think he wouldn't shoot me, but I'd seen crazier things happen. It was the wry turn of his lips, that bit of taunting, that had my gaze narrowing.

No, he had no intention of shooting me. His eyes were as dark as night and focused squarely on me. It was the same look he'd given me when I'd stood upon the bluff, but this close, I couldn't miss the disconcerting intensity. He stood only ten feet or so before me and I could see the dark whiskers on his square jaw. His light blue shirt clung to his sturdy frame, highlighting the breadth of his shoulders. With the sleeves rolled up, I couldn't miss the corded forearms. The tin star on his chest glinted in the sunlight, reminding me of what I was. The daughter of the remaining members of the Grove gang. Hell, to him, I was *part* of that group that had robbed and killed their way across the Montana Territory. He, himself, witnessed me shooting two people in cold blood.

He was good and I was bad. Bad clear through. Bad blood. Bad lineage.

But what was he doing here, eyeing me with an intent to capture, but not put in jail? He'd come after me with a purpose, could have shot me by now, or at least had me cuffed. Why not? He should have been seeing to Father and Travis, but he wasn't. Had they been left where they'd fallen? I'd intentionally aimed to hurt, not kill, although if left for too long, they *could* die. And still, the sheriff wasn't taking them to Simms. He was here. Studying me.

It was difficult not to squirm as he took his time scrutinizing every inch of me. After years of practice, I was used to being patient and waiting to discover a man's mood before I reacted, but couldn't wait any longer. "What... what do you want?" I asked finally, my voice slow and calm. Much calmer than my racing heart, but I still stuttered. Dammit.

I sighed when the red-haired man slowly came around the side of the shanty. I should have expected him, too, but the sheriff's handsomeness had definitely distracted me.

"*We* want to thank you," the second man said.

But his words had me puzzled, especially with the unusual accent. I frowned as he stepped closer... and closer so I had no escape; water behind me and two men in front. "Thank me?"

I lifted my foot to retreat, then realized I'd step into the water.

He grinned and lordy, I swear my heart skipped a beat. Up close, he was tall, an inch or two more than the sheriff. He had a few pounds on the lawman as well, but it was all well-defined muscle. His pants were a dark black, the cut didn't hide his thickly muscled thighs, the narrow hips. "I assume you weren't one of the ones who robbed the bank and decided to take a larger cut."

My eyes widened and I stared at him for a moment. He thought I was one of them? I was a Grove, but I didn't rob the damned bank. "Fuck, no."

"You saved our lives," Hank continued. "You're a really good shot."

"I never miss," I replied, stating plain fact. It was a bold, ego-filled statement, but it was true. "If I aim, I hit my target."

He pondered this. "I'll be sure to keep that in mind. A few words of thanks are the least we can offer."

I nodded, trying not to wonder why my nipples hardened at the dark rasp of his voice. "All right, you've done so." I cleared my throat, glanced down and kicked a pebble. "You can go now."

This feeling, god, this was a new sensation. Nervous. Not *bad* nervous as if I were afraid if I was too loud washing the dishes my father might slap me. Not *horrible* nervous like when Barton Finch had me pressed against the wall and I'd felt every doughy, smelly inch of him.

The sheriff slowly shook his head. "Like Charlie said, that's the *least* we can offer. We'd like to offer you more."

"Oh?" I wiped my damp hands on my thighs.

The sheriff's gaze dipped to my mouth, then lower still to my chest. I glanced down saw the button was undone, parting my shirt more than it should in other's company. The material was damp in spots, but nothing was revealed because of the thick binding wrap. Perhaps he was wondering *why* he couldn't see anything.

He set the gun back on the boulder and approached. Clearly, he wasn't worried I'd somehow get to it and shoot him, perhaps because I'd had prime opportunity to do so earlier and hadn't.

I tipped my chin up when he stopped directly before me. He didn't say a word, only reached up and took off my hat. My braid, which had been tucked up, fell in a thick plait in front over my shoulder.

"Hey!" I said, trying to take my hat from him. He held it aloft. "Give that back."

Instead of doing as I requested, he tossed it onto the ground behind him. "Your outfit is quite the disguise. I'm very glad to find you're a woman," he murmured. He took hold of the bottom of my braid, his fingers playing with the tail below the leather tie, staring, as if mesmerized.

"Oh?" I asked again, licking my lips. He wasn't touching me except for my hair, and yet I *felt* it.

A groan rumbled from him and my eyes lifted to his.

"I've never been interested in kissing a man before."

He wanted to... to kiss me? That answer was obvious when he stepped even closer, his body pressed to me, his mouth hovering just over mine, his lips barely touching mine.

He grinned down at me, which totally transformed him. Laugh lines creased the corners of his eyes, making him seem... nice. It showed his age as well, perhaps a decade or more older than my nineteen years.

"You're right, Charlie," he said, pulling back just a touch. "The men's clothes hide the curves."

If I could feel every hard inch of him, including—gasp! —the thick bulge that pressed firmly into my belly, which wasn't his gun, then he could feel every inch of me as well.

Could feel my curves, that I was, indeed, a woman. Everything I tried to diminish, to keep hidden.

He lowered his head and did just what he wanted. His lips met mine, brushed over them gently, so very softly, completely in contradiction to the ruggedness of the man himself. His tongue flicked out and stroked over my lower lip.

Stunned, I took a step back, my foot landing in the water. With the rocky bottom, I lost my balance. Instead of falling, the sheriff's large arm hooked about my waist and pulled me into him. He grinned.

That wry turn of his mouth set my temper blazing, and I pushed at his chest. "How dare you."

It was like trying to move a brick wall, but was warm to the touch, and I could feel the beating of his heart. He was real, flesh and blood male.

Still, he was just like any other man, pushing his advantage, ready to take whatever he wanted, regardless of my wants. As soon as I thought that, I knew it was a lie. If he were like Barton Finch, he wouldn't have kissed me. That would have been too personal. He'd have groped me. Thrown me onto the grassy bank and had his way, even with his friend watching.

As for my wants, he *knew*. Perhaps it made him a good sheriff, but it seemed he could look at me somehow and see that I desired him, that I longed for his lips to close that last fraction of an inch to press against mine. To kiss me for the first time.

I wasn't resisting him because I was angry with him.

I was angry at *myself*.

Feeling the heat of him, the hot brand of his palm against my lower back as he held me close, the way the tips of his fingers settled dangerously low on my waist, practically cupping my bottom had me all but whimpering. Made me almost swoon like a... woman.

He made me weak. He made me... distracted.

"How dare us? What have we done, sweetheart?" he asked.

What had he done that I could tell him? *You've confused me? Made me aroused? That I liked my first kiss and wanted more... with both of them?* "You've... interrupted my bath."

He looked over my shoulder to the creek.

He released his hold so abruptly, I almost lost my balance once again. I felt... cold and alone without his touch, even though he was right before me.

Slowly, he crossed his arms over his chest and winked. "Don't let us stop you."

His friend, the handsome red-haired man, came to stand beside him. I could get past them, but they felt like a heavily-muscled wall blocking my way.

"I can't... I can't bathe with you here!"

I shivered thinking about the very idea and I continued to cover my fear and confusion by bickering. If I acted tough, perhaps they wouldn't be able to see past the façade to the real me, the one where I was *very* affected by them. That I wasn't scared of them as I was Barton Finch or even my family, but was frightened in a different way. A way that had me fearing they could see all the way to my soul.

The red-haired man, the one the sheriff called Charlie, held out my soap, the little bar I'd set upon the rock beside my gun. Where the sheriff was outright grinning, this one's lips turned up in a small smile. He was equally amused, but wasn't quite so... pushy. He didn't have to be with actions or words, giving me the soap was enough. He agreed with the sheriff. They weren't keeping me from bathing.

"Why not? You watched us at our most vulnerable. We can watch you take your bath."

"I *saved* you from those men," I countered, setting my hands on my hips. Both their gazes dropped with the action.

"And we'll save you from anything that might happen while you're washing," Charlie said. Yes, he did have an accent, proving he wasn't from these parts.

I pursed my lips, narrowed my gaze. "You two are no gentlemen."

They shook their heads slowly and chuckled.

"Never said we were," the sheriff replied.

The other thumbed over his shoulder. "But we're not like the Grove gang. Our intentions are honorable."

My mouth fell open and I sputtered. "Honorable? *Honorable*? How can you be honorable if you intend to watch a woman... a *stranger,* bathe in a creek? Naked." I added the last for clarification.

They both looked bemused now. "How else would you bathe besides naked?"

I rolled my eyes and screeched. Reaching out, I grabbed the soap that was still held out on offer and walked up the creek. Just because I took it from him didn't mean I *was* going to bathe. I just couldn't stare at the attractive man holding the sliver of my favorite soap in his large hand. It seemed so... intimate.

"Very well. I'm Charlie and the sheriff's Hank," the red-haired man said as way of introduction. "Now we're not strangers."

Spinning on my heel to face them again, I gave them a dark, exasperated stare. "You are... brutes!"

They really weren't. I knew brutes and these two weren't them. I didn't know of any other way to behave but to be defensive. To snarl and claw. To fight and push them away.

Keeping them at a distance, even if it meant they didn't like me, was *safe*.

The sheriff tipped his head back and laughed.

"What do you want with me?" I asked, completely confused. Why weren't they upset? Why weren't the calling me names like bitch or worthless female? While he'd kissed me, it was full of intent, but not molestation. Not assault.

"Discovering the perfection that's hidden beneath those horrible men's clothes?" Hank asked. "Besides seeing your naked body dripping wet? Watching your hand slide a bar of soap over your breasts? Seeing your hair long and unbraided? Getting a glimpse of your pussy and wondering if it's wet because of us or the creek?"

My mouth fell open and no words came out. No ire. No rebuttal. I'd never been spoken to in such a manner. Barton Finch had told me what he was going to do to me—*fuck every one of your holes until you're all stretched out and useless*—but that was nothing like the sheriff's words. His made me feel... desired.

The way both of them stared at me, with heated, intense gazes, made me shiver. Made me *want* to strip bare for them and let them look their fill. Somehow, I'd made them look that way, and I felt oddly powerful in a way I never had before.

Charlie put his hand at the front of his pants and... rearranged himself. When he moved his hand away, I could only stare. *There.* Beneath his dark pants was a bulge. No... a very large, very obvious bulge that had the shape of a, of a... of fuck, a lead pipe. It angled upward toward his belt and I would swear it grew as I watched.

"We want you," he said finally.

"I'm not offering," I countered, licking my lips. I had to remain vigilant in my restraint, even if these two were so overwhelming it felt like the creek was rising up and about to wash me away. Earlier, Barton Finch had been all over me and he'd made me feel cheap. Dirty. Worthless. And now, these two wanted the same thing and I felt completely different. Why? I didn't understand.

Their gazes raked over me. "Yes, we can see that. You've done everything possible to hide that you're a woman. Why is that?" he asked, stepping closer, then closer still.

"It's none of your business," I snapped. "I saved your life, you've given your thanks. Now, you may go."

"Being sassy isn't going to help you, love," Charlie said. This close, I could see his brows were a darker shade of red, similar in color to the whiskers on his jaw. His eyes were mesmerizing, an emerald green. I was so used to seeing menace and evil when a man looked at me. With him, it was clear interest, no malice.

The sheriff grunted. "It's only going to get you spanked."

Appalled... and aroused, I spun to look at him, then stormed over to him, poked his chest. "Enough! Leave me the fuck alone." I poked him again—felt how densely muscled he was—then pointed toward the west. "Get on your horses and ride out of here."

I was used to Father turning puce and his veins bulging. I'd never raise my voice to him in such a manner. I'd learned at a young age his temper quickly flared like a lightning strike on a dry prairie. I'd *never* poke him in the chest. Never intentionally rile him.

But the sheriff... his expression didn't change. He didn't even blink when his arm banded about my waist and pulled me tightly into him. I gasped at the hard feel of him. He tugged down the back of my pants. Loose on my hips to begin with since they were an old pair of Travis', they easily slid down my thighs, even with my squirming. His free hand came down on my bottom with a resounding spank.

"Hey!"

"That is not the language of a lady," he said, his voice low and even. He wasn't shouting. He wasn't angry. He wasn't even holding me with aggression. I tested his grip and though it wouldn't relent, it wasn't painful. He wasn't hurting me. Well, my stinging bottom disagreed, but he hadn't hit me like my father had. This was a reprimand of a different kind.

With that one stunning action, I felt equally appalled and oddly comforted.

Regardless, I would not falter before either of them. Through gritted teeth, I said, "I thought it would be obvious to you, I'm not a lady."

That should drive them away. No man—or men—would want me. They wanted a delicate flower who laughed and simpered, preened over a new hat or the pretty color of a new dress.

He spanked me again. "Very well, then I won't treat you like one." He scooped me up in his arms like a bride being carried across the threshold. Instead of entering the shanty and raping me, which had been my immediate thought, he walked up the edge of the creek, bent down and dropped me unceremoniously into cool water. I screeched and sputtered at the sudden feel of the cold water, my already sore, bare bottom resting on the sandy bottom. My knees were bent in front of me, the top of my pants caught on my thighs from when he'd tugged them down. The water wasn't overly deep, it didn't even reach my shoulders, but I was wet and furious.

"You need to cool off, little wildcat." He looked down at me, arms crossed over his chest once again.

I pushed my braid over my shoulder, felt the long tail wet the back of my shirt and tried to catch my breath.

"I should have let them shoot you," I said, my breathing ragged, my hands in fists as I looked up at them. Smug. And dry.

"And I should have kissed you better," he countered. "Maybe that would have tamed you a bit."

4

"Tamed me?" she repeated. "As if that is fucking possible."

I had no doubt she added the swear word out of spite alone, and I tried not to grin. "That mouth would be too busy for talk like that," I added, staring down at the sodden, fuming woman.

Fuck, she was gorgeous. Feisty, confident, prickly. She was the most unladylike female I'd ever met, but also the most stunning. The most appealing. Perhaps because she had no idea how utterly feminine she was beneath the bravado and men's clothing. Her lack of guile, her... innocence was so fucking alluring.

Me, Charlie Pine, of the Meadowlark School for Wayward Boys of London, England, found a woman who wore pants and who chose to—it seemed—live in a dilapidated shack to be *the One*. I'd grown up in a fucking orphanage, not a kind place to be a child. Always hungry, always cold in the winter, threadbare clothing, no love, I'd longed for a family of my own, but never had. I still did. But with a woman who wore pants? Hell, I'd always imagined a mild maiden in pink frocks with fair hair and perfect manners. A sweet thing.

Fuck, look what my heart—and cock—wanted. A pants-wearing, sassy miss who could shoot the wings off a fly and peel paint off a house with her swearing.

My cock was telling me *mine* and my balls were full, heavy and aching to empty into her. I wanted to watch her writhe on my cock and put all that wildness into fucking instead of fuming.

I wanted to claim her forever. Insane, yes. Ridiculous, even. We didn't even know her name. My cock didn't care and neither did my heart.

I'd been in town with Hank when word came the bank had been robbed. The bank with *my* money in it. The money I'd earned breaking my back in the depths of a copper mine in Butte, then eventually becoming part owner. I knew hard, miserable work. I'd grown up with nothing, fought to get to where I was today. I had wealth, but I didn't want it for fancy clothes or fine furniture. I didn't give a shit about any of that. I just wanted the peace of mind knowing that I would never go to bed hungry. I'd never be without a coat or shoes.

Yes, it was the sheriff's job to bring the fuckers to justice, but I'd had to help. Six years with the British army in the tiny middle eastern country of Mohamir had trained me to root out the enemy. No fucking way would those bastards get away with it this time. And since they had robbed within Hank's jurisdiction and were the ones who'd killed his father, he'd been thrilled—and focused—to exact revenge. I was surprised then, when he'd left them on the ground and gone after *her*. Retribution had been at the heart of his every action since his dad died. Hell, if anything, he'd have gone after the third member of their dangerous group. Two down... literally, and one was left standing. Somewhere.

It hadn't been their first hold up. They'd struck Bozeman, then Travis Point, Millerton, Riverdale and now Simms. They'd robbed across the southwest portion of the territory, stealing money from more people than just me. Killing more loved ones than just Hank's father.

I was sure Hank would be the first to admit we'd been stupid riding into that turn below the bluff, practically getting caught with our pants around our ankles and our hands on our cocks. I'd never expected the Groves to linger that close to town, to turn back and sit in wait to finish off those hunting them like coyotes in a hen house. All the other times, they'd made away with the money then fled to whatever rock they lived under to hide out. But cutting us off with the ambush, it took their evil to a new level. They hadn't just wanted money, they'd wanted to kill, too.

They had no conscience. No morals of any kind. They needed to be brought down like the rabid dogs they were.

And yet we hadn't been the ones to do it. *She'd* done it.

She'd saved us... whoever the hell *she* was. Her aim was true, even from a distance. And fuck if that hadn't been hot. There was no doubt in my mind if she'd wanted those two men dead, they'd be buzzard feed right now. Instead, she'd ensured they were injured enough to be unable to flee. Hell, they couldn't even stand up. A gunshot wound, jail and a noose were a miserable fate. Did she know the men? Did she hate them so much she wanted them to suffer? Or had she just been sitting up on the bluff, picking wildflowers and happened to witness our trouble and got lucky firing a gun?

The last was highly doubtful. Her shooting hadn't been luck, it had been skill.

We should have dealt with the Grove men and their injuries, but we'd gotten the money they'd stolen. They could suffer for a while, like they'd made others. This woman was a puzzle I wished to solve. Fuck, more than that. One look up at her on the bluff and I'd known then and there she'd be ours. Hank and I would claim her together. He might not have been in Mohamir with me to learn about their ways of two men claiming a woman together, but he lived at Bridgewater and saw it firsthand with the other couples. Kane and Ian with their Emma. Mason and Brody with Laurel.

Yes, Hank wanted her, too. A good thing, for it was clear she needed two men to tame her.

As for those two members of the Grove gang, we'd have them dragged back to town... eventually. From the wanted posters, it appeared it was Marcus and Travis Grove shot and bleeding. That left the third member still at large. We'd get him, but not today.

Now, *she* was here. Right fucking here and I wasn't letting her slip through my fingers. Her hair, a dark chestnut color, was in a long, single plait down her back. Something for a man to grip and hold onto as he took her from behind. A halo of soft curls which had come loose either clung to her damp skin or caught the bright sunlight, showing off glints of red and gold. She looked a little mussed, as if she'd been fucked a few times. I'd been able to tell her gender as she stood high above us on the bluff, even in the awful clothing. My cock just knew.

Up close, the line of her neck was delicate, even the slope of her brow. Her lips, when not twisted in a frown or grimace, were full and tinged a lovely shade of pink. That had me wondering if other parts of her were just as pink.

My gaze dropped to her shirt, wet and translucent. I could see hints of a pale belly through the clear water, but she wore something beneath the shirt that covered her breasts, and it wasn't a corset. Not even the slightest hint of curves could be seen. It was the fact that her nipples, which had to be rock hard from the cool water, were not visible that had me thinking her body was hidden beneath more than just a men's shirt and pants.

And I wanted to find out. I wanted to discover every secret inch of her. While women were taught to keep their bodies and virtue hidden until they married, this one was taking it to the extreme. I doubted it was for pious reasons either.

Then why?

Leaning forward, I held out my hand. "Come on, love. Out of there."

She looked up at me, then my hand, considering. A smart move because while I did wish to assist her from the water, I also wanted her before me so I could finish getting those pants off of her, and everything else she wore. I wanted her naked.

As Hank had said, we weren't gentlemen. After what had almost happened, it was a reminder life was short, and that we should take what we wanted, to find pleasure and happiness where we could. I knew we'd find both with her, not just in this moment, but for the rest of our lives.

She reached up—knew she truly wasn't afraid of us—and I took her wet hand in mine, tugged, then helped her onto the soft bank in front of me, water sluicing off of her. Her free hand was at the top of her pants, trying to work them up over her bottom. Drenched, she was having little success. Unfortunately, we couldn't see much more than a hint of pale ass since her shirt tail—damn the man she stole it from—was long.

I reached forward to help, but she swatted my assistance away.

"Want to go back in the water?" Hank asked and while she stopped fighting me, she glared at him.

"No matter how much I want these clothes off of you," I said, working the pants up over her wide hips. "I'm putting them back on."

She looked up at me through her lashes, clearly wary. Surprised, even. "Why?"

"Why?" I echoed. "Why am I putting them back on, or why do I want the clothes off you?"

She pursed her lips, considered. "Both, I guess."

"Because when we get you naked, we want you eager and willing, not ornery."

"I'm..." She was about to say more, then shut her mouth. She looked up at me with a hint of confusion. She didn't want us, but yet, she did.

"Willing?" I asked, eyeing her. I wouldn't fuck her, but I would push her to see how skittish she really was. Since my hand was resting on her hip, I had easy opportunity to slide it down inside the front of her pants to see just how willing she was.

She gasped and wrapped her hands about my wrist, automatically attempted to step back because I'd shocked her. A man didn't stick his hand down a woman's pants—not that any other woman wore them.

But the second I found her center, found her folds hot,

slick and silky soft, she gasped, then stilled. She still held my forearm, but was no longer trying to push me away.

"You're eager," I said, glancing down at the surprised look on her face. When I found her clit, all hard and swollen for me, her cheeks flushed and her gaze softened. Blurry. A breathy moan slipped from her lips.

I slipped a finger into her. So fucking tight. She went up on her toes at the entry, but I didn't make it further than the first knuckle, she was that snug.

"A little finger fuck and you'd be willing." I pulled out, circled her entrance that was now dripping, then back in. Eyeing her, I watched every flick of emotion, of surprise, pleasure, awakening. Fuck, she was perfect.

"What's your name?" I asked, gently circling her clit with my thumb as I continued to slide only part of my finger in and out of her pussy.

"Grace!" she shouted, her hips rolling in the most carnal of ways from that light caress.

Grace.

She went lax in Hank's hold. All the stiffness, the prickliness disappeared at her first stirrings of arousal. Instead of sass, all that escaped her lips were sounds of need.

She was remarkably responsive, so sensitive I was sure I could bring her to climax within seconds.

But no matter how much my cock ached to strip those pants off her, toss her on the soft ground and break open that virgin pussy, I wouldn't do it.

Not like this. Oh, she wanted it, but only because it was new. She didn't want *us*. Hell, she was right. We *were* strangers and while we knew we wanted to keep her forever, she didn't know that. Until she came to us begging and pleading to fill her up, we'd abstain from claiming her in every way. That didn't mean we weren't keeping her, but I'd stop. For now.

Inwardly, I groaned when I pulled my finger from her, from her pants. Lifting it to my nose, I breathed in her musky scent, then sucked the digit clean, all the while she watched.

Sweet. Sticky. Like wild fruit eager to be picked.

And if we had to go without, then she would, too.

"Let's go, sweetheart," Hank said, his voice rough with his own need. "The sooner we get to Bridgewater, the sooner we can take care of that pussy."

She went rigid then, remembered herself, remembered she disliked us.

"No fucking way." Her hand went to her pants as if she knew me getting in them could get her to change her mind. "I'm staying here."

Ah, the defiant miss had returned. It only proved that stroking her pussy turned her from a wildcat to a kitten. We just shouldn't stop.

Hank looked to the barely erect cabin. "Here? This shack? Not a chance, sweetheart. You're coming with us."

No fucking way would I let her stay here. Not only could the shack fall down at any time, I wouldn't see her living like this, even for one night. She deserved a soft bed, softer clothes and a hot meal, not whatever hard tack she had in her saddle bag that would only ease the ache of an empty belly. Where would she get more food? Hell, where would she go when it rained, when it turned cold? No fucking way were we leaving her here.

Her dark brow quirked up as she looked up at him. "You're arresting me? I wasn't the one trying to kill you. I *saved* you."

"We're not arresting you," he countered on a sigh. I knew

what he was thinking. We had to pick the most contrary woman in the territory to be ours. She was what I wanted, and I wasn't letting her go. No fucking way. "We're taking you back to Bridgewater."

She frowned, then huffed. "What does that even mean?"

"Don't you know?" Hank asked.

When she was about to continue to bicker about lord only knows what, I'd had enough. I went over to her, leaned down and tossed her over my shoulder.

"Put me the fuck down!" she shouted at my back. I grinned as I walked toward the horses, spanked her ass.

"You're ours, Grace," I told her, giving her another spank. Fuck, that felt good. Not only the feel of her taut ass, but giving it a spanking, too. "Foul mouth, wet pussy and all. We've claimed you."

∼

GRACE

I'D NEVER MET two men who confused me more. They riled me to the point of epic frustration. They also riled me to newfound arousal. I didn't understand them. I had no idea how to behave or act. I had no idea what to do with them, what to say, especially when Charlie took it upon himself to toss me over his shoulder and carry me off. And talk about —and touch—my pussy as if it truly belonged to him.

Father, Travis, even Barton Finch. Those men I understood. They were driven by selfishness and greed. Hatred. They knew about justice, but to them it wasn't shiny like the sheriff's badge. It was tarnished and for the weak. I'd grown up with this perspective, and I had to wonder how I hadn't turned out like them. Somehow, I'd known trouble when I saw it, knew right from wrong. Bad from good.

But that didn't mean it made sense to me. It didn't mean *they* made sense.

Charlie had set me back on my feet before my horse, even offered to help me mount it, which of course I refused with a withering glare. It had done nothing but make him grin and wink at me. I almost felt more naked now without my gun belt and gun, both now in Hank's possession.

Soon after, we'd ridden away from the shanty to Bridgewater, wherever the fuck that was. The sun dried me quickly, but that didn't make me any less uncomfortable. What did I say to two men who I'd saved from certain death, yet who'd spanked and—as Charlie had called it—finger fucked me? Especially since I'd liked it. A man, putting his fingers there... that had been incredible. How had I not known? God, what was wrong with me?

Since I didn't have an answer, I stayed quiet as we rode into Simms long enough to give the satchel of stolen money to a deputy to return to the bank, then to send another along with the town doctor to ride out to collect Father and Travis. I was glad we weren't the ones with that task. Charlie and Hank didn't know I was a Grove—they'd have tossed me into jail then and there if they had—and I intended to keep it that way. No way Father and Travis would keep their yaps shut about who I was, especially since I'd shot them.

Once I was on my horse, I'd taken the time to think. Arguing with them didn't work. They didn't back down. Hell, it seemed to amuse them. I was the one who'd ended up in the creek on my ass, and I didn't want to do that again. More importantly, their strange interest to claim me offered me the one thing I had yet to solve on my own: a safe location to hide.

As a Grove, the last place Barton Finch would go hunting for me would be the sheriff's own home. He'd be stupid to even ride by, let alone knock on the sheriff's front door and ask after me.

While he hadn't participated in this morning's bank robbery—he'd intended instead to have me in his bed, willing or unwilling—he was a fugitive, wanted by the law for other crimes like stage robbery and murder. The only thing standing in the way of the sheriff catching him and putting a noose about his neck was... me. I knew where he lived, but there was no fucking way I'd go back there. I had no intention of getting anywhere near the man again. I felt nauseated just thinking about it.

So I'd spend some time with Hank and Charlie. It would be no hardship, at least on the eyes.

As for the rest of my body... I squirmed in the saddle, the achy feeling Charlie had brought about when he'd touched me so intimately hadn't gone away. In fact, it had gotten worse.

Hell, was I in trouble.

We'd ridden in an amiable sort of silence, letting our horses have their heads as the sun slowly worked its way toward the peaks of the mountains to the west. I was a little lost in the feel of my pussy as it rubbed against the hard leather of my saddle. It had never affected me like this before, not until these two. Until Charlie had touched me. Now... now I wanted to roll my hips and feel... more.

I cleared my throat. "Didn't... didn't you want to arrest the men, take them to town and put them in jail yourself?"

The sheriff, who rode alongside me, turned his head. He tipped his hat back and studied me. "I got what I wanted today."

I frowned, unsure of his words. Did he mean me? He'd

said they planned to claim me, whatever the hell that was. Or did it mean he was content I'd shot the men who'd robbed most of the Montana Territory and they'd be in jail by nightfall regardless who dragged their sorry asses back to town?

He confused me to no end. Especially now when he wasn't trying to rile me.

The sheriff had spanked me. On my bare ass, nonetheless. And it had hurt like hell, but that sting had turned to fire. To heat. To a surprising and strange need. In that moment, I'd hated the man, but at the same time, I'd wanted to jump in his arms and kiss the hell out of him.

It was the strangest combination of sensations. Then he'd chucked me in the creek. The bastard. That had cooled every hint of interest I'd felt.

It hadn't been the sheriff who'd warmed me right back up though. It was Charlie who'd stunned me by putting his hand in my pants. Barton Finch had tried the same thing earlier, but he'd gotten a knee to the balls.

Charlie had gotten me to whimper and moan, practically writhe on his hand. Barton hadn't gotten a finger inside of me, thankfully, but I doubted it would have felt like what Charlie had made me feel. Hot... like liquid fire. Need, fierce and swift, had made me want to ride his finger like a bucking bronco.

I'd lost my mind.

No, when he'd pulled his finger from me and licked it— licked it!—I'd lost it for sure. I wanted him to put it right back! I wanted something that it seemed only he could give me. I didn't know what it was, exactly, but I knew I wanted more of his touch, more even, of the sheriff's spanking.

Fuck, I liked their attention, even if I didn't understand it.

I'd lay low and try to figure out what best to do with Barton Finch at this Bridgewater place with them. I might even let them touch me some more. Because if just the tip of his finger had made me feel like heaven was a place on Earth, then I'd let them do it again. Because the constant shift of the saddle against my pussy wasn't enough.

Over an hour later, we rode up to a house nestled back in a grove of cottonwoods. Compared to the shanty, this place was a copper king's mansion. It was two-story, made of wood with a river rock chimney. It was... lovely. Clean, freshly painted a crisp white. There were even shutters on the windows. Compared to where I'd woken up this morning and spent my past nineteen years, this was... a home. A place for children—ones who were truly wanted—to thrive and grow.

If I had to hide out from Barton Finch, this would be a comfortable place to do it. He wouldn't find me here. There was no connection between me and Hank or Charlie. I'd never even met the men before today. This place, Bridgewater, was far from town, and in the opposite direction of my family's cabin and also from Barton Finch's place. I felt safe here. I felt like I could stay forever. But that was a ridiculous notion. I was the woman in pants. The woman who swore like a drunken miner.

"If you're the sheriff, why don't you live in town?" I asked, glancing from the large house in front of us to the man who just dismounted his horse.

"Because I wasn't planning on being a lawman. I'm a rancher."

I swung down from my animal, patted his sweaty flank.

"But the Groves killed my father."

I gasped, turned on my heel, my braid whipping against

my back. My heart thudded in my ears and I could barely hear what he said next.

"He was the previous sheriff, killed on duty, so I stepped into the role to see them brought to justice." His jaw was clenched tight, his eyes narrowed and his body was tensely coiled as he adjusted his saddle.

Fuck. *Fuck.* Last winter, I'd heard Father say they shot a lawman, but I hadn't known who. I hadn't even known he'd died.

"Then..." My throat felt like dust and I had to swallow hard. Blinked away the quick rush of tears. "I'm... I'm so sorry to hear about your father. I understand why you left them out there, but... but didn't you want to ensure they were behind bars? To see them hanged?"

Charlie took my horse's reins from my numb fingers. "Don't you?" he asked quietly.

The two words were like a loaded weapon, aimed at me and full of intent. He wanted to know why I'd shot them. I couldn't tell them the truth, that I was Grace Grove and my family had killed Hank's father. They'd either toss me in jail for being somehow complicit or kick me off their land. Then I'd be back at the shanty and hopeful I would avoid Barton Finch.

No. I'd stay here for as long as I could. "They were going to shoot you," I replied simply.

It was true. If I hadn't tracked them down after escaping from Barton Finch, if I hadn't found them right *then,* Hank and Charlie would have been murdered. I'd had my chance; I'd had my hatred, and I'd used them both. I'd saved two good men while seeking justice for two bad ones. While I'd aimed and fired, getting justice for *me,* I realized there were so many other people affected by them. Like Hank.

I wasn't sure if Charlie believed me, but he didn't push

for more. I looked to Hank, waiting for him to answer my question. It was one thing for me to be here with them, safe from Barton Finch, but my father killed his father. If he knew...

"They'll get justice." He took off his hat, pinned me with a stare. "And I get you."

5

 RACE

"I assume you wish to have that bath we denied you," Hank said, taking his hat off.

I stared at the dark locks that had been hidden until now. While his hair had curl and fell almost rakishly over his forehead, it wasn't wild like mine. It looked silky and I wondered what it would feel like curled around my fingers. I could now see his strong brow. His skin was tan from the sun and little lines were at the corners of his eyes. He seemed so serious for them to be laugh lines, but I didn't think he was intense all the time. Was he?

I was still caught on what he'd said before. *And I get you.* What did that mean? He didn't want me, surely. Finally, I nodded, remembering he was waiting for a response.

I offered him a polite smile. "Yes, thank you."

"Then we'll take the horses to the stables to be brushed down and fed while you do that."

I looked to Smoky, my horse, the only real thing I had of value... and that I cared about. Charlie patted his neck and I was relieved to know he would be well taken care of. Father and Travis wouldn't hurt one of our horses because they were too lazy to walk. But it didn't mean they were given the best care either.

I retrieved my saddle bag, tossed it over my shoulder. "Again, thank you."

Charlie pointed toward the front door. "Everything you might need is inside."

Lord, they were so nice. They didn't expect me to cook food for them, didn't expect me to do anything but take care of myself. They were tackling the chore of brushing down the horses, feeding and watering them.

I watched them lead the animals away, taking my time to study the two men. The broad shoulders, the taut bottoms, the flexing of their sturdy thighs beneath their pants. Even their long-legged gaits. Somehow, I'd caught their attentions. Well, I knew *how,* but I wasn't exactly sure why. So I'd shot two men for them. It wasn't as if it had taken any effort on my part. I'd told them I always hit what I aimed for. I was glad I'd been there when I had. The thought of them being killed by Father and Travis had me swearing under my breath.

My heart ached knowing they'd killed Hank's father. I could only imagine what kind of man he'd been, law-abiding and justice-seeking, just like his son. I couldn't blame Hank for taking up where the older man had left off capturing the Grove gang.

I felt guilt for being one of them. I *knew* Father and

Travis. Lived with them. I knew where to find Barton Finch. Knew where to end it all for him. Knew how to let him hand the sheriff job to someone else so he could be a rancher again. And I kept him from all of that. The one he'd brought to his house, the one he let bathe in peace... I didn't say a word.

If I were a man, they'd have bought me a whiskey at the saloon. But I was a woman and they'd said they'd claimed me. Now, here I was at Bridgewater.

I saw other houses quite a distance away, a barn and a few other buildings. Was all this land theirs? Was this one large ranch? I was alone and answers would have to wait.

I went inside. The rooms were large and bright, the walls painted the same crisp white as the exterior. Gleaming wood floors were beneath my feet. There was a large fireplace, now cold, in one room I meandered through. It was well-furnished, rich velvets that were soft as I slid my fingertips over it. Smooth wood. Everything was well-kept and spotless.

It was obvious Hank and Charlie were well off. This was not a home of a poor family. I knew that well enough. I circled the ground floor and came upon the kitchen. There were no dirty dishes about, no stench of spoiled food. The kitchen table was scrubbed and there were no scraps of food on the floor. I'd tried to keep up with the housework, to not live in filth and squalor, but Father and Travis had made it almost impossible. I hated being their slave, but I did all the housework more for me than for them. I hadn't wanted to live in a pig sty. I hadn't wanted to live with pigs.

And now I didn't.

I felt as if I were in a dream, a storybook that wasn't real.

But it was.

I looked out the back window over the... was that a pump for water and a sink? I'd heard talk of water being indoors, but had never seen it. I pumped the handle and cool water came out. Leaning down, I took a drink. As I wiped my mouth, I laughed. Inside water.

Through the window over the pump, I saw a creek in the distance. I carried my saddle bag out the back door and made my way to it. The land angled down toward it and a small valley formed and followed the water. When I reached the bank, I stood before a deep pool where large rocks sheltered it from the stronger current. It also had a sandy bottom, and I wondered if this where Hank and Charlie came to bathe. My mind immediately went to them stripping out of their clothing and sitting where I was now. Naked, washing. I took off my hat, wiped my brow. I was still hot and strangely needy.

Charlie had touched me earlier and besides being stunned, I'd liked it and I had to admit to myself I wanted him to do it again. I knew what it led to because I had crude male family members. But I thought it was just fucking, just rutting a cock into a woman. I didn't know there was other things that went with it. The rutting part didn't hold any appeal, but whatever Charlie had been doing was fine by me.

Maybe the creek would cool my thoughts and my body, so after a quick glance about to ensure I was alone, I stripped out of the men's pants and shirt, unwrapping the binding about my breasts. Once naked, I looked down at myself, saw my nipples were hard. I wasn't even in the cold water yet. But my breasts were heavy, achy. So was lower, between my thighs. They'd done something to me back at the shanty. Oh, they'd touched me, but they'd also... bewitched me. I *wanted* them to touch me again. But I wasn't the typical woman. Oh, I had breasts and hips and all that, but I wasn't feminine. I didn't know how to flirt or bat my eyelashes. I didn't swoon or primp. They'd be crazy if they wanted me. Surely, they had eager maidens making calf eyes at them whenever they were in town.

Surprisingly cranky at that notion, I walked into the water. The spring run-off had passed and the creeks were no longer icy cold. Warmed now by the sun and the hot weather, it felt good swirling around my calves. Careful on the smooth rocks, I walked over to the calm pool, felt the sand beneath my feet. I sunk down, then worked the tie off my braid and let the strands loose, using my fingers to untangle the mass. I sighed as it swirled about me on the water's surface. I lay back, floated, closed my eyes and relaxed.

"I'M STARTING to think you have an obsession with creeks."

Spinning about at Hank's voice, I gasped as they approached the water's edge, just as they had earlier by the other creek behind the shanty. Same clothes, same intense stares, same pleased looks that they'd caught me by surprise. This time, I was naked and since Hank just winked at me, he was more than simply *pleased*.

I sat upon the sandy bottom. Water was up to my breasts, but it was so clear that I had no doubt they could see everything. I covered my breasts with my arm and lifted a knee, hoping to shield as much of me from their view as possible.

I was the one caught by surprise for I hadn't been able to hear their footsteps over the sound of moving water. It didn't appear they had any intention of shooting me. They weren't even wearing their gun belts. From the heated gleam in their stares, their thoughts were far from that.

"And I'm starting to think you've got a thing for surprising me," I snapped. I hated being surprised. Startled. Father and Travis liked to scare me just to see me jump. It amused them to no end.

Hank and Charlie grinned, which made me want to snarl at them all the more. They seemed to be enjoying themselves, although they hadn't snuck up on me intentionally. I didn't know them long, but I knew they weren't sneaky. They weren't mean.

I was angry less at them and more at my response to them. They weren't even trying to be... appealing, and I was drawn to them. Just standing there all big and brawny. Then, of course, I thought of what they had done to me standing on the creek bank behind the shanty.

I didn't have an obsession with creeks, but I did seem to be starting one for these two men, and what their hands could do. I'd thought the water would cool me off, but looking at them now... nope.

"There's a copper tub inside," Hank thumbed over his shoulder toward the house.

A copper tub. Inside.

"There is?" I asked. "I... I didn't see it."

"It's behind the stove in the kitchen. Where they're usually kept."

Were they? We hadn't had a tub and if we had, I couldn't imagine stripping bare and washing myself in one. I would have felt horribly vulnerable and I didn't like that, not where my family was concerned.

I'd used a simple basin of warm water I'd heated on the stove and a cloth, washing hastily in my own room. I would wash my hair when there was extra hot water and when Father and Travis were not about. In the summer, I would sneak off to the shanty and bathe in the creek.

That, and this little spot on their property was a treat.

But a copper tub?

"Oh, well, I'm... not accustomed to such an extravagance."

"And we are not accustomed to the extravagance of *you*," Charlie commented. His eyes didn't meet mine, but were focused lower. "Naked."

"Are you done, sweetheart?" Hank asked, his voice lacking the sharp edge I was used to.

I nodded, but didn't move.

"Come on out then."

"Not with you two standing there."

"*Especially* since we are standing here," Charlie countered. "We'll finish what we started earlier."

Hank nodded. "You'd like that, wouldn't you? Charlie's fingers back on your pussy?"

"My mouth this time," Hank corrected.

His... mouth? There? Why?

"I only got a little taste of her earlier. Her flavor's been on my tongue since and I want more. Come on, love. Give me more of that sweet pussy."

I wasn't sure if I should be appalled or eager. It had been hours... *hours*, since I'd met them and yet here I was contemplating letting them not only see me naked, but having Charlie put his mouth between my thighs, too. It wouldn't be like Barton Finch, they'd proved that earlier. They wanted to *give* me pleasure, not take.

Still... I had to say, "This isn't payment for staying here with you."

Charlie's eyes widened and Hank's narrowed, his jaw

clenching. Both took deep breaths and didn't respond right away.

"I'm not sure if I should spank your ass again for thinking so poorly of us, or pull you into my arms for a hug knowing someone did something to you to make you say that." Hank ran a hand through his hair, made the strands stick up every which way as if he'd just rolled out of bed. "Fuck, tell me who hurt you and we'll go make it right."

He'd... he'd go after Barton Finch for me?

"I'm going to eat that pussy because I want it. I want you." Charlie cupped his cock. "See this? It's for you. I want *you*."

"Why me? I told you, I'm not a lady." Maybe he just wanted a hole to wet his dick, just like Travis used to say. If that were the case, they'd have taken me back at the shanty. They didn't need to bring me to their home for that.

"From where we're standing, it's pretty clear you are," Hank said, making me tighten my arm over my breasts. He took the bath sheet I hadn't noticed he'd been holding and opened it wide, held it out for me to step into. "Climb out, sweetheart. We won't hurt you. We'd *never* hurt you."

I studied them again, patiently waiting. "If I didn't want to, would you make me?"

Hank's eyes narrowed even further and if he clenched his jaw even tighter, surely his back teeth would crack. He dropped the towel and turned on his heel to face the house. Charlie winked at me, then did the same.

Slowly, I stood, then got out of the water, grabbing the large cloth and wrapping it around myself. I had no idea if they would turn around and I wanted to be covered as quickly as possible. It was large, but certainly didn't offer much in the way of modesty, especially once it absorbed the water and clung to my skin.

"Decent?" Hank asked.

"Well, I, yes, but—"

They turned.

"—my clean clothes are in my saddle bag."

They stared. I tried to shift and move the bath towel to cover me better, but it was of no use.

6

HARLIE

Bloody fucking hell, she was going to kill me before the day was out. Who the fuck was this woman? Why had she been on that bluff? Why had she shot the Grove men? Why did she wear men's clothing when that gorgeous body would be so beautiful in fancy dresses?

"For every answer, doll, you get a reward," I said.

"Answer?" The white cloth covered her body from the top swells of her breasts to mid-thigh. The material was transparent and didn't hide anything much. Her hand held the two sides together in a white-knuckled grip, but it did little to hide the color of her nipples through the material, the curve of her hip, her long legs. Her hair was dripping down over her shoulder.

"To our questions."

I was impressed Hank hadn't pried before now. It was

obvious she was hiding things, and not just her lush body. Did they matter? No. I wanted her no matter her story. The way she acted around men, she hadn't been with one before. She wasn't married. In fact, she behaved as if she didn't like men, that perhaps one had gone too far with her. The way she responded to my finger fuck earlier, it hadn't been rape. Thank fuck. If someone had hurt her, we'd take care of it. Of him. No one would harm her again.

I dropped to my knees before her. Startled, she took a step back, but I hooked my hand behind her thigh. Her skin was chilly and damp, but so soft. Smooth but when I gripped it, I felt her firm muscles.

"Stop that," she said, fighting me at first, but realizing she wasn't going to win, placed her free hand at the bottom edge of the bath towel to ensure it stayed down. I'd get it off of her soon enough.

Of course, she didn't know that stripping her bare was to her own benefit. We intended to give her the pleasure we'd denied her earlier. It was apt we were on the bank of a creek again. A bed would have been nice, but I'd make her come outside just as easily. And I wasn't wasting another second carrying her back to the house.

"Answers, doll. Or Hank may throw you in the water again," I warned, even though I had no intention of her getting out of my hold now.

"He's the one who got me wet in the first place," she grumbled, giving Hank a dark look.

Out of the corner of my eye, I couldn't miss the grin that spread across his face at her words. "Sweetheart," he began. "I hope so, but are you still wet after all this time? I'll find out soon enough."

Clearly, from the frown on her face, she didn't understand the secondary, and more carnal, meaning of those words.

"Why were you up on that bluff earlier?"

She stiffened at the question, pursed her lips. "I was riding by and saw the men pointing their guns at you. It's hard to miss the star on your chest." She tilted her head toward the badge on Hank's shirt. "They needed to be stopped."

"And you decided to do that. You have pretty good aim."

"I don't miss."

She'd answered, so it was time for a reward. Leaning forward, I put my mouth on a nipple and sucked, even through the damp fabric.

Gasping, she tugged at my hair. I wasn't sure if the slight pain was to pull me away or to hold me in place. "What are you, oh god."

I grinned, then gave the berry tip a little tug before I sat back on my heels again.

She stared at me wide-eyed and a little confused.

"No one's touched you before, have they?" Hank asked.

That wasn't my next question, but I did want the answer.

She shook her head. "No." The one word came out on a whisper. "Why... why are you doing this?"

"This is us giving thanks," I said, probably only adding to her growing confusion as I reached up and tugged the wet bathing towel from her fingers. It lowered to her waist, caught there on her damp skin. She was bare to the waist and lovely. Fuck, stunning.

"By seeing me naked?" she screeched, her arm going across her chest once again to cover herself. Slowly, I reached up and lowered it, then held both her hands out at her sides so we could look at her.

She was skittish, nervous even, but she wasn't fighting

like a woman who didn't want it. She might argue with us, but she wasn't fearful or screaming no. There was no panic, only the last vestige of her bravado. She wanted it, but didn't know exactly what *it* was.

"By making you come," I clarified.

"Come?" she questioned.

Oh fuck. I looked up at her, the way a little V formed in her brow, the way her full lips pursed. A pretty pink flushed her cheeks and I wiped away a drop of water from her cheek. She had no idea to what I spoke, which meant she was a virgin in all ways. As if she'd been tucked away in a French convent instead of gallivanting across the Wild West.

She might have made a practice of bathing in a creek, but had done so alone. No longer. We'd see every inch of her. Touch her. Kiss her, lick her. Taste her. And soon enough, fuck the prickliness right out of her.

I wanted to ask her more questions, but they could wait. I had a naked, virginal woman standing before us. It was time to discover what she liked, what made her hot. What made her scream our names.

I looked at her, saw her staring back at me through her dark lashes. Waiting. Barely breathing. With my hands on her hips, I pushed the sodden bath sheet down until it fell to the ground at her feet.

I couldn't help but groan when her pussy was revealed. While she had a dark thatch of hair on her mound, it couldn't hide her plump pussy, the hint of her inner lips peeking out or the hard, pink pearl that was swollen and eager for us. Droplets of water slid down her inner thighs, but I knew she'd be slick with arousal, too.

"Charlie!" she cried, glancing from me to Hank and back. I liked my name from her lips, but I longed to hear it in a different tone, when she was breathless and screaming it in her pleasure.

Hank stepped up behind her, banded an arm about her waist, held her firmly against his chest, one hand cupping a plump breast. She began to resist then, for he'd been the one earlier to spank her sweet ass and toss her in the creek.

"Shh, let him look," he murmured in her ear, then kissed the delicate swirl.

"But—" she began.

"We won't hurt you, love," I said, my hands sliding up and down her thighs in a reassuring gesture. Her damp skin was silky smooth, and I felt the firm tone of her muscles tense and quiver. "You're safe with us. Your body knows it even if your mind is resisting."

"I've never—"

"We know," Hank said, his nose nuzzling down the line of her neck. She probably didn't even realize when she tipped her head to give him better access. He brushed her wet hair to the side and over one shoulder. I watched as beads of water dripped from the ends and slid down her breast.

Goose bumps broke out over her damp skin and she shivered. She couldn't be cold, not with both of us touching her, the heat of the sun quickly drying her. With my palms still on her thighs, my thumbs settled at her center, stroking over her pussy. She gasped, jerked in Hank's hold. As I touched, then parted her so I could see her very center, Hank whispered words of encouragement, told her specifically—and plainly—what I was doing, all the while licking and nipping at her ear.

A whimper escaped her lips.

"You're so beautiful," I said honestly.

She *was* pink. So pretty with the slick folds, her clit all but begging me to touch it. And then there was her little virgin opening, never before seen by a man, let alone fucked. Though I'd pushed my fingertip into her earlier at the other creek, given her a few little strokes, it was nothing like what I had planned. This time it wouldn't be just one finger and though mine would be the first, Hank's would be the last.

With the tip of one of mine, I circled that untried entrance. So hot and wet, slippery with her body's eagerness for us.

"Oh, dear lord." She bucked, then gasped. Her inner walls kissed the top of my digit, as if trying to pull it in. I obliged, the tight, hot feel of her surrounding up to my first knuckle.

Hank kneaded her breast, played and tugged at the hardened tip with his fingers. She began to writhe and shift her hips, uninhibited. Wild. *Fucking perfect.*

She looked down at me with those dark eyes, this time there was no flare of anger, only heat. Confusion. Need. "Please," she whispered.

I worked my finger into her a little more, her juices easing my way, although she was so fucking tight. We'd have to take her time preparing her for our cocks so we didn't hurt her.

"Please, what?" I asked. "Please more of my finger in your pussy, or please play with my breasts?"

Fuck, they were a vision, so pale that I could see the thin blue veins beneath the surface, with pert, large nipples. The tips were hard and pointed toward me, but the outer area had little bumps I wanted to feel against my tongue.

Why she kept them so tightly covered so they were hidden completely, I didn't understand. Whatever she wore, she would never don it again. Hank and I would have to debate if she would even wear a corset. She was too lovely to be confined.

"Both," she begged and I grinned. I found her clit, making her hips roll in the most carnal of ways from that light caress. Oh, she was a responsive thing.

Our Grace.

Her body was well muscled, with long, lean legs, full hips, a narrow waist that tucked in without any need for a corset. And her breasts... I could stare at them all day. I could watch as she responded to the way my friend touched her. She wasn't petite, only a few inches shorter than Hank, even barefooted. She wouldn't break if we took her roughly. She'd proven her spirit was strong, and I doubted she needed kid gloves. No, she needed two strong men to handle her.

"Grace." Hank murmured her name as he reached about and cupped both of her breasts again, testing their weight, kneading them. The tight nipples, which poked out between his thumbs and forefingers, thrust toward me and my mouth watered to lean forward and lick one, then the other. Suck on them until I felt her pussy juices dripping down my palm.

I pulled my hands away from her, then stood. We could make her come quickly, just a few more brushes of my finger over her clit and she'd go off like TNT in a silver mine. We wanted her hot, needy and all but begging for the pleasure she didn't even understand. To be at our mercy, to crave us and what we could give her. Only then would she come.

I had had to kiss her. *Feel* her against me. Tugging her in close, Hank let go and I set my mouth upon hers. She gasped and I used that opportunity for my tongue to find hers, to explore and learn.

She moaned against my lips and went up on her toes, two signs that Hank had moved his hand to play with her pussy from behind.

I settled my hands between us, cupped and played with her breasts. It didn't take long for her to moan and writhe from our attention. She pulled her mouth from mine, rested her head back on Hank's shoulder and her eyes fell closed. I watched her face as we pushed her into her first climax, my fingers tugging on her nipples and Hank working her pussy and clit in just the right way.

He held her up when she came on a scream, her mouth open, her skin flushing from her cheeks, down her neck and over her breasts. She was so beautiful, so passionate.

When her legs gave out, Hank scooped her up and laid her out on her back in the soft grass. I didn't wait for her to recover, only dropped to the ground between her thighs and put my mouth on her.

Her flavor burst on my tongue and I lapped up all her juices. She was dripping, her arousal glistening on her thighs, pussy and even the tight swirl of her little asshole.

I couldn't help but grin as I flicked that taboo spot again with my tongue. Oh, we'd have more than my tongue there. Soon, she'd have our fingers and even our big cocks deep in that back hole.

It was that flick, over the crinkled opening that had her eyes popping open. She came up on her elbows and looked down her naked body at me, her knees splayed wide.

"What are you *doing?*" she asked, her voice rough and breathy.

She was fine sprawled naked beneath the bright sunshine, a man between her parted thighs, but had issue with me licking her there.

"Making you come again."

"With your mouth?" she asked, stunned.

I wiped my mouth with the back of my hand. Super slick. "Lay back, doll, and I'll give it to you."

"But... there?"

My hands cupped her taut ass and so it was easy to press a thumb against her slick back entrance. "Here?"

"Yes, there. That's not... you shouldn't—"

"I should. Trust me. You're going to love it."

Lowering my head, I flicked her clit with the tip of my tongue as I kept my gaze on hers. I did it again and her eyes fell closed. Once more and she dropped back onto the grass, giving up.

I rolled my hips into the hard ground, trying to ease the ache. Her pussy was wet, open and eager for a cock. She'd be tight, completely untried. I *needed* it.

Glancing up at Hank who stood above, watching, I knew it wasn't the time. We'd get her so sated with orgasms she'd have no eagerness to be without us. We'd fuck her, but we'd get a ring on her finger first. It was obvious some fucker had hurt her. We wouldn't be like him. Like that. We'd give her pleasure, but we'd only take ours when *she* was ours. We wouldn't take that pussy until then.

But I could lap up all her honey and make her call out my name. And so I did. From asshole to clit, I worked her, fingers and tongue, taking her to the brink and stopping. Again and again until she was a sweaty, writhing, *begging* mess.

"You like it when I play with your little asshole, don't you, doll?"

"Charlie, please!" she cried, her hands tangled in my hair and trying to push my face back between her thighs.

I chuckled. "Say it."

"I like it!"

"Good girl. Now you can come."

One flick of my tongue on her clit and she screamed, gushed all over my chin. If this was how she was from just a little oral play, I didn't think I'd be able to survive when I got my cock into her. Or when both of us took her at the same time.

7

RACE

"If they've brought you here, they've claimed you," Emma said, with a sly turn of her mouth. She was a beautiful woman with black hair and striking blue eyes that were only accentuated by the similar color of her dress.

I paused in my folding of napkins, which I'd never done in my life. The task seemed silly since everyone was going to place them in their laps anyways, but I lived with men with manners no better than wild dogs. Perhaps she took one look at me in the clean pants and shirt I'd taken from Travis and figured I needed a simple task. I could cook quite well actually, since I'd been the one expected to do it, but Father and Travis certainly weren't worthy of folded napkins.

I looked to her down the long table. She was slicing strawberries and adding them to a bowl for dessert. Around us were a few women who lived at Bridgewater. Ann, Laurel and Olivia, who were busy with various meal tasks. The scent of roasted chicken made my mouth water.

After the creek, I'd put on my clean clothes from my saddle bag, pants and shirt I'd stolen from Travis, but not the binding over my breasts. Hank and Charlie had taken one look at the long strip of old fabric and had refused me that. We'd walked the ten minutes to another house, this one belonging to Emma. I'd met her husbands—yes, she had two, Kane and Ian—and the husbands of the other women. They'd gone off with the children, a mix of toddlers and babies yet to walk, to play outside.

In the hour since we'd arrived to help prepare for dinner, I'd learned quite a bit about Bridgewater. It wasn't Hank and Charlie's ranch, but a number of them, everyone working together as a community. The land they owned as a group was vast, and growing. So were the families. With each woman having two men, and Olivia having three, it was no wonder they were having lots of babies. This arrangement was something they'd discovered in some far off country called Mohamir. I hadn't been out of the Montana Territory, so I'd never heard of it. But most of the men were British military who'd been stationed there, including Charlie. That was why he had a funny accent. He was from England, like Kane and a few of the other husbands I'd met. Laurel's Mason and Brody and Olivia's Rhys and Simon.

What was I doing here? This morning, I'd been taken to Barton Finch and left, as payment. I remembered the feel of his groping hands, the fetid scent of his breath. I knew what real men were like, how they treated women. Oh, Charlie and Hank were bold ones, taking liberties with me. But while I was skittish, they'd had my consent. Barton Finch had not.

Since then, I'd shot my only living family and left them for the law. I was in a strange place with people who were... nice. I was talking with women who treated me as a friend —a strange situation in itself—about two men who had not only said they'd claimed me, but had touched me carnally and in ways that had brought me amazing pleasure.

I knew nothing about Charlie. Or much about Hank, for that matter. And yet they'd seen me naked. Touched me naked. Hell, Charlie'd had his head between my thighs and his mouth—

I closed my eyes. They made me feel like they were truly interested in me. Perhaps it was naïve to consider that, for I knew men to be shallow and only want a woman for one thing. I had no doubt Hank and Charlie wanted me for that *one thing,* but they hadn't done it. They hadn't fucked me. They talked about it. I saw their hard cocks pressed against their pants, but they hadn't even tried. They'd touched me. Given me pleasure while they'd found no relief.

It made no sense. I cleared my throat, realized Emma was waiting for me to reply to her comment. "That was a word they used. Claimed."

All four of them smiled at me as if it were a good thing, this *claiming.*

They were polite, genteel ladies. They were married. Had children. *Wore dresses.* What these ladies must think of me, how they must wonder how I, a woman dressed like a man, could snag the interest of two handsome, rich men like Hank and Charlie.

Ann laughed, turning my attention her way. She held up a potato masher and had a firm grip on a large, steaming bowl. "They're a bossy bunch, the men of Bridgewater. When they see the woman they want, they claim."

"Why don't they just use the right word? I mean, it's fucking, right?"

They stared at me wide-eyed, then Emma shook her head. "Well, there is fucking. Definitely, but a whole lot more."

"*More* than fucking?"

I thought of the *claiming* they'd done at the creek. Both of them. There had been no fucking involved. I was the only one who'd been naked.

"Oh, look at your face, I can tell that they've already done so," Laurel added with a laugh. I knew my cheeks were bright pink, for they felt hot.

"No, they haven't, I mean... not that."

"Fucking?" Emma asked. Her black hair was pulled back in a loose bun on top of her head, but she blew out a breath to move a curl off her forehead.

I nodded.

"Just because I look all prim and proper doesn't mean I don't say the word, or know what it means," she replied, setting the bowl on the table before her. "I have two husbands."

"I have three," Olivia said. "Trust me, I know all about cocks and fucking."

"Yes, but Hank and Charlie aren't my husbands," I countered, not taking the time to think of Olivia surrounded by three men all trying to get their cocks in her.

"Yet," Laurel added, passing behind me to put shucked peas into a pot on the hot stove.

"They're honorable. They won't take your virginity until you're married. Anything else... it's to show you how much they desire you. They must have shown you what it would be like without their cocks in you," Emma offered. It was as if she were speaking of the latest styles of hats with her calm tone, not fucking.

"I married Robert and Andrew the day we met," Ann said.

"I woke up naked and in Mason and Brody's bed the morning after they rescued me from a blizzard," Laurel added, clearly trying to show me I wasn't the only one who had men who had touched them carnally and directly after meeting. "While they didn't fuck me before we married, they did stroke themselves and cum all over me. Marking me."

I set my hands on top of the napkins. They didn't really need to be folded. But I did need to hear these ladies' stories. I wasn't as... wild as I'd thought. I wasn't broken or crazy or a harlot. They eased my mind, a little.

"I was rescued from a virgin auction, married to Kane and Ian, then fucked within an hour," Emma said. "What did they do with you, Grace? It can't be anything we haven't seen, done or wanted."

I looked between them, all eager to hear more. "They touched me."

"Your pussy?" Olivia asked. "That feels so good."

"Your ass?" Laurel added. "I never imagined liking it, but... I do." She grinned wickedly.

I shook my head.

Emma frowned. "They didn't touch you?"

I swallowed, took a deep breath. I was not accustomed to sharing my thoughts and definitely not my feelings. And on this topic? Never. "They touched me and Charlie put his mouth on me. Between my legs."

All four of them sighed.

"But..."

"Yes?" Laurel asked. Her blue eyes were alit with eagerness.

"He put his tongue... there. Where you like so much."

She all but squealed and clapped her hands together. "Oh, if you liked that, just wait until they open you up with a plug or a cock."

"There?" I asked, stupefied.

All four of them nodded. I squirmed at the possibility, then stilled, realizing I was a little crazy for wanting something so... dark. And yet, Laurel said Mason and Brody fucked her... her ass? And what was a plug?

"But we're not married," I replied. "Surely that's not proper." I'd only come to Bridgewater to get away from Barton Finch. To hide. These ladies were talking about fucking and plugs and having cum all over them.

"You're claimed," Emma clarified with a decisive nod. "Same thing. They're keeping you. And as for proper..." She looked down at the men's shirt I wore. "You don't seem the type to be worried all that much about *proper.*"

My mouth fell open. "Keeping me?"

The idea made my heart race. I was *wanted.* Truly wanted if Hank and Charlie were keeping me. It made no sense though. This was all happening so fast, in less than a day. I didn't even want to think about how they'd feel about me when they knew who I really was. But I wasn't my family. Yes, I shared the same name, but I hadn't robbed a bank. I hadn't killed anyone, let alone hurt them. I wanted to be claimed or kept or married by a man. I hadn't considered two men until now. And yet, the idea had merit. I felt things with them I never imagined. Not just the pleasure they wrung from my body, but safety. Comfort. I felt cherished. *Wanted.*

"Look at me! Like you said, I don't even look very feminine. I don't even own a dress."

Laurel smiled, came by and patted my shoulder. "If Charlie's licked your virgin asshole, then he's seen you out of your clothes. Trust me, they all like their women better without clothes. They'd keep us naked if they could."

The other women nodded their agreement.

I stared at them all, wide-eyed. Somehow, this was so much more than I'd expected. Never did I imagine I'd be talking about something so... so dark and intimate with a group of ladies. A passage from the Bible perhaps or even a recipe for peach pie. But being licked in such a place?

Hank and Charlie *were* so much more than I imagined. I didn't want to be stuck with two bossy men. I had just shot two. "I met them earlier today. They couldn't possibly—"

"We couldn't possibly what?" Hank asked, coming in through the open back door. He had a little boy in his arms. Around three or so, he seemed thrilled to be carried. I noticed then he had Hank's tin star pinned to his little shirt.

"Shewiff Hank made me depty!" he said, grinning from ear to ear.

With a ruffle to the top of his curly head, Hank set the boy down. The child ran to his mother, Ann, who gave him a kiss on top of his head. Seemingly content with that loving gesture, he ran back toward the door.

Charlie had entered as well, but stepped out of the boy's path and grinned down as he dashed by. My heart rolled over at the sight of those two with the boy. Neither had blond hair, but I could imagine them with a child of their own. A boy with dark hair like Hank or red like Charlie. They'd teach him to shoot, to catch frogs, to be protective of baby sisters... fuck, I was dreaming too much. But they were good men. I knew it. I felt it. They would be good fathers. They definitely wouldn't be like mine.

"What couldn't we possibly want, sweetheart?" he'd asked again, not forgetting the question.

"You couldn't possibly want to... to marry me."

Hank's open expression narrowed, focused on me. His jaw clenched. Charlie crossed his arms over his chest. "Why ever not?"

A laughed then. "Look at me." I waved my hand toward the other women. "Look at them. Why are you being so stubborn about this?"

"Why are you?" Charlie countered. "We aren't marrying you for your pants. Besides, you weren't wearing them down by the creek."

I flushed hotly, even though I'd been just speaking about what we'd been doing down by the creek.

He grinned. Winked.

"We claimed you," Hank stated plainly, as if that explained it all.

"See?" Emma asked.

I didn't look her way, but kept my gaze fixed on Hank.

"Yes, but I'm just here with you to—"

Charlie quirked a brow. "Just here to what?"

Hell and damnation. I couldn't tell them the truth. "I just... I just met you and you're talking marriage. It wasn't like Charlie gave me any option to come here when he tossed me over his shoulder," I grumbled.

The ladies chuckled, obviously not surprised by their stubbornness. I had to wonder how many of them had been carried about like a sack of potatoes by one of their men.

Hank grinned and came to stand beside me. He was so much taller and I had to tip my head back to look up at him. The way he looked at me, so different than earlier, made his features soften. Oh, his jaw was still square and sharp, his nose still long and straight, his brow prominent, but it was his dark eyes that now held... warmth. It made me soften just a little, too. "Sweetheart, you want it, too."

I frowned, those soft edges gone. Not one to be told my mind, I countered, "I met you this morning."

"Yes, but you want us enough to spread those thighs and let Charlie lick your pussy. I had my fingers inside you, felt your maidenhead that we'll be taking later. You wouldn't have let just anyone do that."

I sputtered at his talk in front of the other women. "No, of course not."

"You'd allow it for your husbands," he continued.

The women remained silent, but they were smiling.

"Yes, but—"

Hank grinned wickedly. "Good."

I stared at him. Wide-eyed. How had I been talked around to marriage? "I'm not marrying you!"

I'm just staying at Bridgewater until I figured out how to deal with Barton Finch. What I'd done with Hank and Charlie didn't mean I wanted them forever. Did it? Just because my body had responded so intensely... it didn't mean... what did it mean?

"We'll have a shootout," he offered. "You, me, Charlie. If one of us wins, we marry."

I stood and they stepped back. I paced the room. For the first time in my life, I wanted to cry. Not because of them, but because of me. "I'm surprised you touched me earlier."

I turned and looked up at both of them. They had matching frowns. "Why is that, love?" Charlie asked in that smooth accent of his.

"Because you can't be attracted to me. Look at me." I pointed to my pants, then my shirt. Travis' clothes. The clothes of a man who'd planned on killing both of them. "You didn't even ask me to marry, you made it a wager."

"Do you want us to get on bended knee?" Hank asked.

I rolled my eyes, tossed up my hands. "I don't know! But I just don't understand why you want *me.*"

The men glanced over my shoulder, and I watched as the ladies quietly went outside. Once we were alone, Hank stepped close, cupped my jaw and rubbed my cheek with his thumb. The touch was intimate and gentle, and I couldn't help but tilt my head into the caress.

"It's not because you saved our lives," Hank said.

"It's not because your pussy takes like sweet honey," Charlie added. Hank turned his head and stared at him. "What? I'm not marrying her for that, but I won't mind tasting it every day for the rest of my life."

Hank shook his head in disbelief, but he didn't disagree.

"We want to marry you because we knew the instant we saw you up on that bluff, gun smoking by your side," Hank said.

"You thought I was a man."

"My cock knew. There's nothing you could be except all woman. Pants and all."

"We want you because you're not all fancy and prim," Charlie added. "We want you because you're a little wild. Untamed."

"You spanked me because of that," I reminded.

"I spanked you because you swear like a bunch of randy ranch hands." He paused. "Sometimes there's no explanation why a man wants a woman. Why she's The One. It's just... lightning."

Lightning. Out of everything they said, that made the most sense. It was completely ridiculous, but so was what I was beginning to feel for these two in such a short time. I couldn't believe how I reacted, how I responded when all I'd had before them was hate and anger toward men.

Charlie took my hand, lifted it to his mouth and kissed the knuckles. The gesture was sweet and yet it made my nipples pebble. His green gaze was fierce. "We don't know much about each other, but time will fix that. I grew up in a London orphanage. It was… worse than anything you could imagine. I escaped by entering the military. There, I found a family of sorts. A band of brothers, but I longed for a wife. Children of my own. But I had nothing. No money, no way to support and care for a wife properly. I came here to America, to Bridgewater, to build that dream."

He turned our hands over so I could see his scarred knuckles and I felt the thick callouses against my palm. "I worked hard and built the means to support a family. But I hadn't found the right woman."

He kissed my knuckles again, rolled my hand over and kissed the inside of my wrist. The brush of his lips there had me gasp, for it was just as intimate as when he had his head between my thighs.

"Until you."

The words were powerful, but it was the intent gaze, the honesty I saw in his expression. He wanted me. He wanted a life *with* me. And yet, I'd only intended to come to Bridgewater to hide from Barton Finch.

He wanted *everything* and I unevenly only wanted his protection. Even that wasn't true. I didn't need that from him. I could take care of myself. I just wanted a place to hide. Not him, or Hank.

Was that true now? Was that all I desired now? Even after a few short hours, things had changed. No, *I* had changed. I liked the way they looked at me. Touched me. Spoke with me. I liked the way they made me feel, and not just when I was naked and they had their hands on me. They didn't belittle how unladylike I was. They didn't shame me. They didn't hit. Quite the opposite, in fact. They put me first. Honored me. Valued me. Fuck, they truly wanted me.

"Do you want us to get down on bended knee or do you want a shoot out, sweetheart? Pick the right one because it's a story you'll tell our grandkids."

God, was I really considering marrying them? Fuck, I was. No, not considering. I *wanted* to marry them. But I didn't want to outright say it either. They were running roughshod all over me, and I was not going to stand for that. I refused to go from one house to another where two men bossed me about.

The waited for my answer. Two handsome men. Virile, rugged. One dark, the other with lovely red hair like fire. Solid, sturdy, stalwart. They were also *good*. And they wanted me. They wanted me, flaws and quirks and all.

They somehow *knew* me, because... a shootout? He knew I could hit a target. I'd never seen either of them fire a weapon before. Did I want the romantic gesture or did I want to beat their pants off?

I smiled, for they really did understand me. A whole life with Father and my brothers—my oldest one, Tom, had been shot and killed in a robbery a few years earlier—and they barely paid any attention to me, knew my wants, my dreams. They knew nothing about me except I was a woman and I served them food and cleaned their house. I wanted a real home, a real family with Hank and Charlie. "Shoot out. Definitely a shootout."

8

Hank

I'D BEEN SO DRIVEN, so focused on capturing my father's killers. Ever since I received news he'd been shot, point blank and in cold blood, I'd wanted justice. I'd even taken the drastic step of taking over as sheriff. It had meant time away from Bridgewater, staying in town and sleeping at my father's house, the one I'd grown up in. Without him there, it had felt empty, and it had made me realize my life was empty, only filled with the justice I wanted so fucking badly.

I hadn't appreciated my father's interest in defending the vulnerable until he was gone. Only when we lowered the pine box in the ground had I felt vulnerable myself. My mother had died birthing me, leaving my father to care for a newborn alone. It had been just the two of us ever since and he'd done a good job. But one bullet and I'd become alone. I'd become victim to men who ruthlessly and without any morals killed a lawman.

I wanted retribution and revenge. I wanted the Grove gang caught.

And now, we had two in custody. I should have felt elation. Felt that justice was a little closer to being served. I did. Fuck, yes. But it wasn't bringing Father back. He was still dead. Still gone. I was satisfied to know they wouldn't be hurting anyone else.

Marcus and Travis Grove would have been dragged back to Simms by now, sitting in the jail cell. The doc would have patched them up enough to live until they were sentenced and hanged, probably gave them each a bottle of whiskey to dull the pain.

They had a week, I guessed, until they were dead. As sheriff, it was my job to see it done.

I'd follow through, but without the judge in the area, there was nothing to do but wait for him to stop at Simms on his circuit. I had no interest in waiting in town, sleeping in my father's house. No fucking way. I had something else to fill my time. *Someone.*

Grace.

Perhaps it was Father looking down on me and laughing. Just when I'd gotten exactly what I'd wanted, the long-awaited justice, I got something else I wanted more. Was I a kid deciding which sucker candy to choose at the mercantile? Could I be greedy and want both?

Fuck, yes.

The Grove men would hang, not because it was what I wanted to avenge what they did to my father. It was because it was what they deserved. Did that mean I deserved Grace, too?

Our paths had crossed when she saved us, and in that instant, she became mine.

Ours. There was no question. No doubt on my part. Or

Charlie's. We had completely different backgrounds, growing up on two different sides of the world. And yet here we were in the same place together. Wanting the same thing.

Grace.

I still didn't know her reasoning behind shooting those men. There was a story there, and we hadn't given her much opportunity to share it. We'd get it from her. She'd have no secrets with us.

We'd made it plain as the sun in the sky that we had claimed her.

Obviously, based on what I'd heard of her conversation with the other women, she hadn't known what that meant exactly. I'd have thought Charlie's mouth on her pussy would have been informative enough.

Obviously not. But I wasn't fucking her until the vows were said. She'd just have to believe our words.

What I had learned about the wildcat who had claimed me... yes, she'd claimed us in return, was that the more I told her what to do, the more she rebelled. Even when getting her to marry us. We gave her a choice, albeit one where we were content with both outcomes. Us on our knees asking for her hand in marriage like a man who wooed a woman, courted her. Or a shootout.

Of course, Grace chose the shootout. She wasn't used to romance and fancy words. She wasn't used to being wooed. We'd cherish her, adore her. Give her everything she could ever want, but I didn't think it would ever be a fancy straw hat with lace and ribbons.

Dinner, of course, was delayed. Everyone wanted to watch since Charlie and I had shared the story of how we met, of how she'd saved our lives. It wasn't often a wedding occurred depending on who was the sharpest shooter.

Mason and Brody set a long line of potatoes on a fence a

distance away. They were small targets, but I had little doubt she'd miss. I knew her to be that good. Her targets on the Grove men weren't random. She'd chosen them intentionally. Aimed and hit her mark. Both times. I didn't know why she chose them, there and then, but I would. For now, I was content to watch her do it again. Because oddly enough, it was hot as fuck. It was going to be difficult to keep from tossing her over my shoulder, carrying her to the stable and taking her virginity with a nice hard fuck. I'd claim her nice and dirty and deep like I wanted. Like I knew she'd love. Then I'd watch as Charlie gave her even more cock, more pleasure.

Grace stood between me and Charlie, each of us holding our preferred weapon, loaded. Our future wife shouldn't be between us ready to fire a gun. It wasn't what I'd envisioned. It wasn't the kind of woman any of the other men at Bridgewater had. But I didn't want a woman like Emma or Laurel. I wanted Grace, just as she was, secrets and all.

"Each of you will get six shots," Kane said, taking on the impromptu role of official. The others—Emma, Ian, Brody, Olivia and her husbands—stood behind us for safety. Mason and Laurel sat with Ann, Robert and Andrew closer to the house with the children to ensure they didn't run into the line of fire.

I looked to Grace, who was gazing at the potatoes. Focused. Her hat was off, her long hair wild and pulled back in the thick, familiar braid. She still wore men's clothing, but her breasts were unbound—that long strip of fabric would be burned—and outlined in the large shirt. I could even see the hard tips of her nipples poking against the worn material. I knew what they looked like, what they felt like in my palms. *Fuck*. Once this competition was over, her hair would be unbound, her clothes on the floor of my bedroom and Grace in my bed.

"The most hits wins."

She glanced up at Charlie, then me.

He held out his hand. "Ladies first."

She rolled her eyes and checked her weapon.

Turning to the side, she raised her right arm, weapon pointed. She was calm, her breathing slow and even. Her arm was steady as she exhaled, then fired.

Then again, and again until all six shots were used.

One potato remained on the top of the fence.

Closing her eyes, she swore under her breath, which made my lips twitch in amusement. She knew she'd get her ass spanked for such language, and it would not be a hardship to mete out another punishment. Fortunately, the next time I spanked her, I'd be able to fuck her directly after. Then she wouldn't think it a punishment at all, for she'd come, and hard.

"I thought you never missed," I murmured.

She looked to me and just shrugged. I narrowed my eyes and wondered. Had she missed on purpose? If so, why—

"Bloody hell, woman, where did you learn to shoot like that?" Kane came over, slapped her on the shoulder, albeit gently, and grinned down at her. "We could have used you in the British army." She smiled up at him. The fucker. She didn't smile like that at me. Then again, he wasn't claiming her either. He wasn't the one who seemed to make her more contrary than less. Yes, that was my job and I would be eager to see that fire and sass aimed right at me, just like her gun.

"Hands off, Kane. You've got a woman of your own," I told him. Why did he need to touch Grace when he had Emma? She was a beautiful, lusty woman. There was no doubt she was satisfying her two husbands.

Kane's gaze shifted to mine and he slapped me on the back and laughed. "Glad to finally see you claimed, Sheriff."

He was vexing me on purpose. I knew it, but I didn't care.

"My father taught me to shoot," she replied, ignoring the way I practically pissed on her leg to stake my claim. "He taught my two older brothers. I watched and practiced when they weren't around."

This was an interesting bit of information. I glanced over her head at Charlie. It was more than we'd gotten from her on our own. It was a start.

"He should be proud of you," Kane said.

She stiffened. "No. That wouldn't be what my father thinks of me."

Kane's expression didn't change when she answered, but it made my blood boil. From the crispness of her voice, she didn't like her father at all. "And your brothers?"

She sighed. "One's dead," she replied as if she were speaking of the weather. There wasn't a hint of sadness in her expression. "The other... we don't get along."

"Do we need to ask your father for your hand?" I asked. I was a gentleman in some things. I'd pay my respects to her family as was expected, but no matter his answer, I was claiming her anyway.

Her chin tipped down and she stared at her boots. "No. I'm on my own now."

Charlie cocked a brow, but said nothing. "My turn to shoot, love."

Kane stepped back.

She looked to him and he winked, then turned his attention to his target. He shot one potato easily, then the next. He lowered his arm, looked to Grace. "Did I tell you I was a sharpshooter in Mohamir?"

He aimed and fired again. And again. Like Grace, he missed one.

"A tie," Kane stated, although that was obvious to everyone watching.

My turn. There was no chance I was losing this competition, especially when the stakes were so high. I wanted Grace as mine.

I adjusted my stance, raised my arm to point my gun at the edible targets, then glanced at Grace. She was biting her plump lower lip, realizing she just might be married tonight. Well, not just might.

I looked at the line of potatoes, fired one after the other, exploding six in a row.

I tossed the empty gun to Kane, then hooked my arm about Grace's waist, pulled her into me. Brushing a curl back from her face, I said, "Charlie might be an expert military sharpshooter. But I'm the son of a Montana Territory sheriff."

I kissed her then, fierce and possessive. This time, when my tongue flicked her lower lip, she opened for me. Kissed me back. Hot, wet, sweet and the little moan that escaped sealed her fate.

Grace was ours, fair and square. "Robert," I called when I finally lifted my head. "Pull out your Bible."

9

 RACE

"Wait!" I shouted, panicking. I wasn't ready to marry them at this moment.

Actually, I was, and that was the reason I'd called out. I *shouldn't* be ready. I needed time to think. They'd been like a tornado. I'd heard about one that had struck east of Billings a few years back. Strong, swirling winds and total devastation. I felt like I'd been tossed about, at least my emotions anyway, all day long. It was like they were a fierce storm that had blown into my life and changed it. Turned my path, my entire way of life upside down in a matter of hours.

I needed time.

I needed—

"I need a dress!"

Charlie and Hank stared at me. So did Kane, Ian, Mason and the others.

"Of course, you do," Emma said, approaching her husbands holding a little girl with the same dark hair as hers. Ellie. She was beautiful and a little shy, clinging to her mother. When she was close enough, she reached her little arms out for Ian, who took her and tossed her up in the air. Her squeals of laughter made me relax. A little.

"Every woman should wear a dress for her wedding."

I was thankful for her intervention, for she was justifying my words.

"Fine. We shall return to the house and you can put one on," Hank said, as if it were so easy.

"I don't own a dress."

"Borrow one," Hank added, looking to the women of Bridgewater.

Ann and Laurel were too short. Emma was closer to my height, but her bust was much larger. Olivia was much curvier than I.

"She must have a dress of her own, Charlie. Something special to remember the day."

"We'll give her something to remember the day," Hank replied and I felt my cheeks heat, knowing to what he was referring. He'd said they wouldn't take my virginity until we were married.

"Two somethings," Charlie clarified.

"It is too late today, but we can find a ready-made one at the mercantile," she added.

"Love, let them resolve this themselves," Kane told Emma, wrapping an arm about her waist from behind and kissing the top of her head.

Hank took my hand and led me away from the group. Charlie followed.

"You are scared," he said.

My mouth fell open. "I... I believe I am, but not of you." I fervently looked to him, then Charlie. "Not of either of you."

I wanted to have him call Robert and his Bible over and become theirs. Why did I *want* that? Why did I want to stop bickering and just say yes? "I... met you a few hours ago. I need to at least... at least—"

"Yes?" Charlie prodded.

"I need a night to sleep on it."

"To change your mind?" Charlie asked. I saw the little V in his brow, the worried look. He thought I might reconsider, might not want to be their wife.

I shook my head. "No. *No.*" I meant it. I had no intention of second thoughts. "You're right. You've claimed me."

The tension slipped from his features, his jaw unclenched. Those lips that had kissed me, had been on my pussy turned up into a small smile. "That's good, love."

It felt good to know I'd eased his mind, to be the one to offer him happiness. It was odd, this sensation, knowing that me wanting to be with him made him content.

"It seems this claiming is more important than a wedding."

Hank nodded. "We've agreed. To me," he tipped his head toward Charlie. "To us, that's enough. You're ours. Since two men are marrying you, it is not conventional, or legal. But we will do it nonetheless."

"You will marry me, love."

I flicked my gaze to Hank and he nodded in agreement. I wondered why he wasn't bothered by the fact that he and I wouldn't be legally wed. He was the sheriff. The one who believed in black and white.

"You will have my name, but today, when we first saw you, you became ours."

I felt light, like I could float. Was this happiness? Was

this love? I had no idea but I... I liked it. And I wanted it more. I wanted it always.

"I have no intention of changing my mind. But I need a moment to breathe. To think. The two of you are overwhelming."

Both of them grinned wickedly. "And we still have our clothes on."

That was definitely what I was afraid of.

"You're correct, sweetheart. When we get you between us, you won't be thinking at all."

I swallowed, then squeezed my thighs together, knowing that was true.

Hank nodded. "All right. We will marry tomorrow after you go to town for a dress."

Tomorrow. It was as if waiting an extra day was a huge burden, especially since I'd known them less that twelve hours.

"You can sleep between us."

I sputtered and held up my hand. "If I'm in a bed between you, I hardly doubt you'll let me sleep."

Charlie winked. "Smart woman."

"She can stay here tonight," Emma called.

We hadn't walked too far away from the others, and they were definitely a nosy bunch. I liked it.

I tried not to let my relief be too evident. Hank and Charlie were like a stampede, running roughshod over anything in its way. They weren't thrilled at the idea of me being out of their sight, but nodded nonetheless.

I looked to Emma. "Thank you kindly."

Charlie turned my head with a finger to my chin, forced me to look up at him. "Know this, love. You'll be in the dress long enough to say the vows. Then it'll be stripped off of you."

I swallowed, for I didn't need to see the honest intensity in his look. I only had to hear the carnal promise of his voice.

"IF YOU LAUGH, you know I can shoot you," I grumbled, sliding the curtain between the mercantile and Mrs. Maycomb's living area at the back.

I'd come to the store with Emma and Ann first thing with Quinn, one of the ranch hands, escorting us. We were in Travis Point, the town with the *better* mercantile for ladies ready-made wear. I had trusted their judgement on this, and I now looked down at myself. Pale blue gingham covered me from neck to wrist to waist, then belled out in a full skirt that was large enough to hide my unladylike boots.

"We will not laugh," Emma said through the curtain.

I wasn't so sure now that insisting I wear a dress to my own wedding had been a good idea. I felt ridiculous. I had never worn a dress, let alone gingham or pale blue in all my days. It was practically suffocating me with how trim the fit was, and I wasn't even wearing the wrap around my breasts. *That* had been snug, but it had been beneath my clothes, hiding my figure, not accentuating it as this dress was. I didn't have much of a mirror, Mrs. Maycomb only had a small one that she held in her hand, but I'd been able to maneuver it about to get some idea of my appearance.

"Are you going to stay back there all day?" Ann asked, then I heard the two of them laugh.

"I'm glad you're enjoying yourselves," I grumbled. "I'm not."

"Come out, Grace. You're going to look lovely."

I could run out the back door, but that wouldn't do me

any good. I'd still have to face the women when I wanted a ride home. *Home.* Did I now think of Bridgewater as my home?

I had barely slept last night for all the thinking I'd done. I wanted Hank and Charlie. I did. I was, perhaps, just as crazy as them. As everyone at Bridgewater for they all wed in haste.

But every couple there was happy. The women were adored and protected, the men doted upon and loved. If that was crazy, then I wanted to be a part of it.

I was. I just had to walk out from behind the silly curtain so the ladies could see me in a dress.

Thank goodness Hank and Charlie were in Simms, checking on the prisoners while I was shopping. I'd consistently pushed thoughts of my family from my mind. I hadn't wanted them in my life and they weren't any longer. I'd ensured that. I was getting everything I ever wanted.

"Grace!" Emma called.

I sighed, swiped the curtain back and stepped into the back corner of the mercantile.

Ann gasped and clapped her hand over her mouth. Emma squealed and came over to me and wrapped me in a fierce hug, then stepped back. She looked me over, perhaps even more thoroughly than Hank and Charlie had.

"You're beautiful! Those two men of yours are going to swallow their tongues."

"And die of blue balls before they even get inside you," Ann added.

I blushed and felt something blossom in my chest. Hope, perhaps? Hope that they'd still like me even though I was wearing something that made me different? Wasn't that what I had always wanted, to be different? To not be a Grove?

"You think so?"

Ann nodded, her blonde curls bouncing. "It fits you perfectly. You have to take it and a few others."

It was easy for her to speak of dresses. She was wearing one. A pale yellow color that showed off her hair and her three husbands had no doubt she was a woman.

I gave her a funny look. "One dress is plenty. I only need one to marry Hank and Charlie."

They shook their heads in unison.

"When you get back to Bridgewater and they get one look at you, they're going to rip that one to bits in their eagerness to have you," Emma vowed. The idea of Charlie and Hank seeing me and being overwhelmed with desire for me, enough to ruin a dress, made me feel powerful. Being feminine, for the first time, felt like I had some control, that I was somehow bewitching to my future husbands. Was it like that? Did I, with just being me, have power over Hank and Charlie?

"More than one is required," Ann agreed. She looked to Emma. "Let's go see if they have a pink. That would look pretty with her complexion."

"Pale yellow?" Emma countered.

"Let's go see."

"I'll change my clothes and be right out."

They turned back to me as one. "Oh, no. You may fetch your other clothes, but you are wearing that dress out of the store." Emma stomped her foot along with it and gave me a look that probably worked well on recalcitrant children, or stubborn husbands. They walked off toward the ready-made dress table, leaving me alone at the back of the store.

I huffed, then spun on my heel to retrieve the pants and shirt I'd worn into town. I took one step and someone stepped into my path.

"Well, looky here. The perfect disguise."

My heart leapt into my throat. Barton Finch.

"I wouldn't have recognized you if you'd kept your mouth shut. That sassy tongue of yours gave you away. Bitch."

His gaze raked over me and he licked his lips when they affixed upon my breasts. They were unbound and I was without a corset. I wasn't going to glance down to see if my nipples were poking out. "There's more to you than I thought."

I cringed at his breath, his leer.

He'd had me cornered like this just the day before, but we'd been alone and at his cabin. Alone. Now, we were in the mercantile and Ann and Emma were at the front with Mrs. Maycomb.

"Don't make me scream," I said.

"Don't make me kill those two fine ladies."

I froze at those words. He grinned.

"Couldn't help but overhear. Bridgewater, huh? That the place where two men get to fuck a woman together. Sounds like my kind of place." He looked me over again.

He now knew where I'd been. Knew where Ann and Emma were from.

"You wouldn't like it. People bathe," I countered.

He grinned showing off his yellow teeth.

"What's this about marrying two men? Did I hear you mention a Hank? Do you mean Hank Baker, the sheriff?"

I'd become accustomed to hiding my every emotion from my family. If they knew something excited me, like a stray cat, they shot it. If they knew something bothered me, they'd continue to pester me with it. They'd left the front door open, allowing flies in the house all summer long just because I'd told them it annoyed me. They were assholes.

I'd known it before, but after meeting all the men at Bridgewater, it was confirmed.

And Barton Finch—

"Smart idea, Grace. Shacking up with the sheriff to save your neck. And marrying him?" He laughed. "Fuck, woman, you've got guts. You must be a better fuck than I thought if the sheriff can get past your name. That pussy must be incredible."

I tipped my chin up, stayed silent, for I wasn't going to respond to his crude words.

Guilt swept through me, fierce and strong, because I'd thought just that the day before. But then I'd stopped thinking it entirely because I *wanted* Hank for him. I wanted Charlie, too. I wanted them as a woman wanted a man, not a Grove wanting protection. I'd forgotten about my life for a few hours and had hoped. Had wanted. Had actually had something more.

"Did you disguise your name, too? What do you think will happen when I tell him who you really are?"

With Barton Finch standing before me, I knew it was all over.

"As if you'd get anywhere near the sheriff," I snapped.

He didn't respond to that. Instead, he asked, "Think your neck will snap when you're on the gallows or will you swing and jerk for a while until you strangle and suffocate?"

Bile rose in my throat at the words. They were true. I would hang right along with them. I was Grace Grove.

"What do you want?" I whispered.

"I got a bank to rob. Word's spread about the two Groves who got shot and are in jail."

He didn't know I was the one who'd shot my own family.

"I can't do it alone. Now I've got you."

I shook my head. "No. I haven't done it yet and I won't

start now."

He looked over his shoulder to Emma and Ann who were by the front window trying on straw hats. A slight shrug of his shoulders brought up his rank body odor. My nose wrinkled, but I didn't move. I didn't dare.

"Seems to me I'll have to make a little visit to Bridgewater. Late at night." His hand settled on the butt of his gun at his hip. "Maybe I'll do a little shooting of my own."

My biggest problem now wasn't being raped by him. He was now a danger to those who had taken me in, become instant friends. They'd made me one of their own unconditionally.

But there was a condition. They wouldn't want me if I were an outlaw and Barton Finch was forcing me to it. But I would rather them all hate me than see them hurt.

"When and where?" I asked.

He grinned again. "Like I said, smart woman. Carver City Bank. Noon tomorrow. After, you'll come to my cabin. We'll spend the night getting to know each other."

I didn't say a word. The idea of being in his company now, let alone spending the night with him made me nauseated.

"You and I are going to get along just fine. Don't worry, I won't mind a broken in pussy, but I bet that ass is virgin. I'll take it and make it mine. Since you kneed me in the balls yesterday, I'll be sure to tie you up nice and good before I get on you. That way I can take my time with you." His hand came up and he grabbed my breast. I didn't move, but I did flinch, for his hold was rough, painful. Nothing like the way Hank had touched me the day before. I stepped back.

Lightning quick, he gripped my wrist and I tugged, trying to pull it free.

"Fight me. I like it," he growled.

I stilled, pursed my lips and tried to slow my breathing, to calm myself.

"Carver City Bank. Tomorrow. Don't show, I know where to find you. You decide to give your men the proverbial knee to the balls and get on the nearest stage out of town, I'll still kill them."

"And if I tell the sheriff?" I hissed.

"Tell that sheriff husband of yours everything. You'll end up in jail beside your father and brother. Those at Bridgewater will still end up dead." He pulled his gun out, checked to see if it was loaded, then put it back in the holster, which had me wishing I'd stolen every weapon the man owned. "Or don't tell him. Fuck, I wish I could see his face when he finds out his soon-to-be wife is an outlaw. Happy wedding day."

He turned around and walked away, laughing.

I had no idea how long I stood there, staring at nothing. Thinking. Trying not to cry.

I wouldn't do anything to get those at Bridgewater hurt. Barton Finch didn't toss out empty threats. I couldn't tell Hank or Charlie about this. I was going to the gallows no matter what I did, but I'd see them alive and safe. I'd saved their lives once; I'd save them again.

I had until tomorrow. Between now and then, the time was mine. My life was mine. I could be who I wanted. I could be married, to two men. I would try to forget everything else and enjoy one day as a wife, one day where everything was right in my world. Where everything was good. I had one day to be happy, then it would be over.

I'd no longer be Grace Grove. I'd be Grace Pine and though not legally, I'd also be the sheriff's wife. Then... I'd become what I'd always vowed never to be... an outlaw.

Soon to be dead.

10

HARLIE

"Fuck me," I whispered, standing beneath the tall cottonwood tree outside of Kane, Ian and Emma's house. Hank was beside me, both of us in our Sunday best of black suits, white shirts, vests and ties. While we were in the shade, the sun was warm, but I barely noticed. Grace was all I could see as she walked toward us, escorted by Robert.

My cock, which had been semi-hard all day, went instantly hard at the sight of her in a pale pink dress that fit her like a glove. It was the first time—besides her being naked—we'd seen her curves. There was lace edging at the high neckline and at her wrists, making her appear almost dainty. With her hair pulled back, not in a braid, but in a bun at the nape of her neck, she was a vision. She was Grace, but at the same time, a different person entirely. I didn't care what she wore, or hell, if she wore anything at all.

It was the perfect female beneath the pink fabric and lace I would marry.

She glanced at us, both of us, with a tremulous smile. I realized then, she was nervous, not to wed us—well, perhaps that, too—but about her clothing. She'd said she had never worn a dress before.

I couldn't help but smile back. Beam, even. Fuck, if those bloody bastards who ran the orphanage could see me now. They'd told me I'd never amount to anything, that I was worthless. I might now be a simple rancher, but I had everything I ever wanted walking toward me.

She was the woman I'd always wanted but had been waiting for. She was the start of the family of which I'd dreamed. She was what I'd worked my bloody fingers to the bone for in those wretched copper mines. She was the sun and the moon and I was the stars. Shakespeare had it bloody right.

When her eyes met mine, I let her know with a look alone that I was ready for this. For her. I was ready to marry her and make her mine. Yes, we'd claimed her, but God and everyone at Bridgewater would know she was mine forever. She'd take my name. She'd be Mrs. Charles Pine.

Fuck me.

Her hand came up, her fingers playing with the lace at her neck. I was proud of her, doing something so profoundly different. For us. It made my heart pound, my palms sweat, to know that she put in such an effort, even at an emotional risk for herself, to do so.

It had been a long night without her, even though we had yet to spend one night *with* her. I hadn't slept well, thinking of her, of how we'd touched her, how she'd responded. Fuck, I could still taste her sweet pussy on my tongue. I'd wanted to use my hand and ease the ache in my balls, but I'd declined, saving all my cum for Grace. I'd fill her with it until we were all sated. I didn't know how long that would be. Days.

When we'd returned from Simms, confirming the Grove men were alive—albeit ornery and mean—and behind bars, we'd immediately gone to Kane and Ian's house to see Grace. The women had returned from the mercantile and had frittered about Grace like birds, but they'd refused Hank and I her presence until now. Kane had slapped me on the back and sent both of us to clean up for the wedding, stating if he let us in the house, he'd be sleeping in the stable for a week.

Hank nudged me in the back when she stood before me, prompting me to take her hand. I did, then met her upturned face. I wanted to reach down and shift my cock to make it more comfortable in my pants, but that wasn't going to happen until I got them off. Soon.

"Ready, love?" I whispered.

Hank moved to stand on her other side, putting her directly between us, right where she belonged.

Her dark eyes were bright and eager, her smile was genuine, the pink in her cheeks showed her excitement.

"Yes, I'm ready to be yours," she replied. She looked to Hank. "Both of you."

She was ready. Hank was ready. I was ready. So was my cock. I turned to Robert. "The short version."

And in about two quick minutes, I was cupping her face with my hands and kissing her. When Hank cleared his throat, I lifted my head and she turned to kiss him next.

We didn't even let the others do more than offer us quick congratulations. Grace was ours and we weren't wasting a second finally claiming her. I tossed her over my shoulder and carried her back to the house, not putting her down until we were in my bedroom.

I held her waist as she regained her bearings. She didn't look fierce in soft pink, or with her hair up in such a dainty fashion. I hadn't worried overmuch that we'd be too rough with her. Yesterday. But now, seeing her all soft curves and sweet perfection, I worried we'd be too much for her, that we might possibly hurt her.

"Don't be afraid, love. You might be getting two big cocks in that virgin pussy, but we'll take care of you."

She looked up at me through dark lashes, and I was ready to see apprehension or even a touch of fear a woman felt taking her husband for the first time. Grace had two, so...

Instead of lip biting and hand clenching, thinking of the Queen and all that, Grace flung herself into my arms and kissed me. Hard. Wild. As fierce as she was.

Holy bloody hell.

GRACE

I WAS SO HAPPY. Truly. I felt light. Carefree. Loved. I'd never felt like this before. But standing between two men who'd vowed, in front of their closest friends, that they would honor, cherish and love me, protect me with their bodies, love me with those bodies as well... I knew they weren't lying.

Unlike Father or Travis, or the bastard Barton Finch, they weren't talking shit to get what they wanted. They weren't thinking only of themselves.

Charlie and Hank definitely wanted to fuck me. Their constantly hard cocks were obvious proof of that, but they'd put a ring on my finger first. I was Grace Pine now.

I swallowed back all feelings of my own perfidy by giving them not my true name, but my mother's maiden name. I'd married Charlie as Grace Churchill, not Grace Grove. But the vows I'd said were honest. I wanted them. *Both* of them.

I hadn't fought when Charlie carried me back to their house. *Our* house. I'd relished the feel of his eagerness, his desire to make me his in all ways. I'd seen Hank's legs as he followed, and I knew he was just as eager. Just as ready.

I had one day to be Mrs. Charlie Pine, to be Hank's wife, too, in everything but name. Tomorrow, they'd hate me. Tomorrow, I'd be in jail where I belonged. Tomorrow—

No. I wouldn't think of tomorrow. I'd think of today. Of now. Of them. If I were going to hang beside Father and Travis, then I wanted one day of perfection. One day of happiness before I died.

And so I didn't allow Charlie one moment of worry. One moment of being careful with me. I wanted him. I wanted Hank. I wanted it all.

So I threw myself at him. Kissed him with all the pent-up need I'd felt since they'd left me at Emma's house the night before. There was no time for modesty or questioning. They would never hurt me. They'd only give me pleasure.

For an instant, I'd stunned Hank. Then he wrapped his arms about me and kissed me back. A growl escaped as I boldly thrust my tongue in his mouth.

Once again, he set me on my feet and his hands began to roam. Not just his hands, Hank's too. My dress was unbuttoned with haste—a few even flying off because of our untamed eagerness—and off my shoulders, down my arms and in a puddle at my feet all the while Hank's mouth was on mine.

Their hands continued to roam, to caress, for I was naked except my stockings and boots. I was the one to break the kiss when both men's hands were on my pussy. I was wet for them and they slid easily over me. I gasped, for it felt so good. Heat spread through me, like mercury slipping beneath my skin.

Both men sank a finger inside me, filled me at the same time. It was so tight, they stretched me wide.

I gasped, clung to Charlie.

"So fucking tight," Hank murmured as he kissed along my shoulder. "Don't worry, we won't take you here at the same time. Charlie will fuck your pussy while I fuck your ass." His slick finger slid to my back entrance, to the place where Charlie had licked. The fingertip circled, then pressed in until I had both men inside me.

I cried out, for it felt so good, yet odd. Both holes were stretched and while it burned, it reminded me that they were claiming me, that I belonged to them. I wanted it all, to know what it was like, to be completely taken, completely claimed. I didn't want them to hold back, to keep themselves in check.

"More," I panted.

Charlie leaned down and took a nipple into his mouth, sucked hard and I felt it in my pussy.

I tangled my fingers in his silky hair, held him in place. I felt him smile against my breast.

"Smothered by your glorious tit. The perfect way to go," he said, looking up at me.

Playful and handsome.

"More," I breathed. "I haven't seen either of you yet. I want you bare."

Hank's finger slipped from me and I heard the rustle of clothing.

"If you let go of my hair, I'll oblige," Charlie said.

Releasing him, he stood and worked off his jacket.

My pussy felt empty and was achy and needy for them. I was so slick I was wet along my inner thighs. I felt silly standing in my boots and stockings, I sat on the edge of the bed, removed them, all the while watching Hank and Charlie. The room was sparsely furnished, a big bed for Charlie's large size, a dresser with a mirror above it, a chair in the corner. Two windows, open to the warm day, faced out of the front of the house. The sun streamed in.

The more they bared, the more I wanted them. They were so different, in temperament and in body. Charlie was bare chested, with a line of red hair that started at his navel and traveled down to the base of his cock. And what a cock! Long and thick, it was a ruddy pink color with a broad head. He stood proudly with muscled legs that made his cock jut out. He gripped the base in his large hand, stroked up the length, circled the tip with his thumb.

Hank moved to stand beside him. Just a touch shorter, his shoulders were broad, a narrow waist that tapered into a muscular belly. He, too, was well endowed. His size was comparable to Charlie's and my inner walls clenched, wondering how either of them would fit.

Their fingers had been snug, but those cocks...

Hank grinned. "Don't worry, sweetheart, your pussy was made for us."

I nodded and licked my lips. They both groaned.

"You see us. You can touch us, too," Charlie added.

I stood, walked over to them, set one hand on each of their chests. They remained still as I touched them, roved over them. Felt the heat of their skin, the play of their muscles, the quickness of their breathing. Charlie continued to stroke himself as Hank's cock bobbed toward me.

Curious, I touched Hank's cock and he hissed out a breath, his hips rocking forward.

"What about me, love?" Charlie asked, dropping his hand away. I gripped him, too. "Fuck," he hissed, and his eyes fell closed.

"Show me what you like," I said, looking up at them. Their eyes were dark, their jaws tense. Every line in their bodies was taut.

Charlie's hand settled on top of mine in a firm grip and his gaze was fierce. "This will be over too soon if you keep at it."

I frowned, not sure what they meant.

"You're eager, sweetheart. You want our cocks?" Hank asked.

I nodded, licked my lips.

That action had Hank grabbing me about the waist and tossing me on the bed. When I landed, he crawled over me, the hard prod of his cock on my inner thigh.

Leaning down, he kissed me. Sweetly, yet thoroughly. When he lifted his head, I was panting. "Let's get you ready."

I writhed beneath him. "I'm ready."

He shook his head, kissed me again, then along my jaw. He worked his way down my neck and to my breasts, kissing them, licking the hard tips, even nibbling the curve of soft flesh. He moved lower and lower still and I parted my thighs so he could settle between, just as Charlie had done by the creek the day before.

I came up on my elbows and looked down at him. "Charlie had a taste. My turn."

His mouth on me was different than Charlie's. He was

gentle at first, barely touching me with the tip of his tongue, then he licked me in one flat pass of his tongue.

I dropped back onto the bed, stared up at the ceiling. "Fuck," I breathed.

"Soon, love," Charlie said, sitting on the edge of the bed, his hands going to my breasts. It was as if he couldn't *not* touch them.

Between Hank licking every inch of my pussy, flicking my clit, and Charlie playing with my breasts, I came. It was fast, quick, hard and had me panting, my skin slick with sweat.

"More," I said, making it my mantra today. I wanted everything. No holding back, no waiting. I didn't have time to tease or for them to play, so I rolled my hips. When Hank lifted his head, his mouth slick and shiny from my wetness, I said, "Fuck me."

He came up over me again, kissed me. I tasted myself. "See? Such a sweet pussy. Ready for it to be mine?"

I nodded, ran my fingertips over his jaw, felt the rasp of his whiskers.

Using his knee, he nudged my thigh wider and settled in. His cock slipped over my folds and the head caught at my entrance. "You're mine, Grace." He slid in, not stopping, not giving me time to adjust to the thick feel of him, until he was embedded all the way.

I shifted my hips, gripped his upper arms and breathed. He was so big and I'd never felt so full. So snug. I gasped at the intrusion. It wasn't painful, but it was... uncomfortable.

"Look at me," he said and I realized I'd closed my eyes.

His dark gaze met mine as he held himself still, his body supported on his hands. "You're perfect, sweetheart. So hot. So tight. So wet. You're everything we want."

He pulled back then and I gasped, eyes flaring wide. That hadn't hurt. That felt good.

"Again," I whispered.

He pushed in and I cried out.

"Like having your pussy broken in?" Charlie asked. "Fuck, seeing you get taken for the first time is too much."

I turned my head, looked to Charlie. He was watching us as his hand worked his cock quickly, the grip snug, looking where Hank's body joined with mine.

Hank pulled back so he was almost completely out of me, then plunged deep. Again, then again. The sound of wet fucking and ragged breathing filled the room.

The feel of it, the way his cock slid over secret, carnal places inside me made me hotter and hotter. Every time he bottomed out in me he rubbed against my clit.

"I'm going to come," I said, digging my nails into the curve of his ass, feeling the muscles go taut as he pumped.

"Come, sweetheart. Come all over my cock."

He didn't slow down, just took me hard. Fast. This wasn't a gentle coupling, an easy transition into marital relations. No, this was pure need. Pure fucking. I wouldn't have it any other way.

When the pleasure was too great, too much for me to handle, I let go. I screamed and clawed, writhed and begged. Gasped and wrapped my legs about Hank's waist.

He took me still, his motions losing their smooth cadence until he stayed deep. Groaned. I felt the heat of his cum fill me, knew that I'd made him lose control, that it was my body he'd found his pleasure within.

I smiled, lost in bliss.

When he caught his breath, he pulled out, a thick gush of cum slipping from me. I was too sated to move, but a gentle slap to my pussy had me gasping, my eyes flying open.

"My turn, love. Look at you, all sweaty and happy. Well-fucked. I love seeing your pussy all swollen and pink, cum slipping from it."

Charlie was the one who liked filthy talk. So did I. A hand hooked about my hip and he pulled me over onto my stomach, then tugged me up onto my knees.

I looked over my shoulder at him. His gaze was on my ass, on my pussy I knew was on full display. He didn't say anything more for it seemed just looking at me had pushed him to the edge.

He moved behind me, gripped my hips and filled me.

"Grace. Fuck, you're perfect," he whispered.

I tossed my head back as he took me, this position so different and he was able to go so deep. My inner walls rippled around him greedily.

His palm struck my ass and I gasped, the sting of it turning to even more heat. "You ready, love? Time for me to take you for a ride."

"Yes," I said, then nothing more as he fucked me hard. Deep, jolting me forward. He pulled me up so I sat atop his thighs, his hands cupping my breasts. I could do nothing but take him, let him use me for both our pleasures.

Hank flopped down on the bed, his head on the pillows, one arm up and behind his head as he watched. His cock, while just spending deep inside me, was still hard.

His cum eased Charlie's way, made him slide in and out so easily, even as my body adjusted to two cocks in a row.

His hand found my clit, flicked and played with it, coated it with the cum that had slipped from me.

I was so sensitive, so primed, I came again. Then again.

Charlie pushed me back down so my ass was up, my cheek on the soft blanket as he used me for his own release, finally filling me with a harsh growl and firm grip of his hands.

As he fell onto the bed on the other side of me, sandwiching me between him and Hank, we were all worn out. I fell asleep to their hands on me, the heat of their bodies pressed into mine.

They woke me while the sun was setting to fuck me again. Then again once night had set in. It was as the sun was rising that I rode Charlie's cock, straddling him like he was a wild mustang and there was no way to tame him, just to ride him until we both came. Hank slid a hand down my back, slipped his thumb into my ass and I rode both of them.

"Soon, sweetheart, we'll fuck you together," he murmured, but I was screaming my release.

Instead of slipping into sleep once again, I lay awake listening to Hank and Charlie breathe, to feel their hands resting on me, watching the sun creep across the ceiling as my husbands slept on either side of me. I was sore, my body well used. I had their cum all over me, my skin damp with sweat. I'd found the pleasure that was had in a loving marriage. I had the devotion and attention of two men.

But it would all end, for I had to meet Barton Finch. I had to keep everyone at Bridgewater safe. I'd had the night I always wanted, had the men I'd never imagined. I was married.

It was time to walk away. Time to keep those I loved safe. I'd had it all... if only I could discover a way to keep it.

11

Hank

"Where is she?" I asked, wiping my eyes and realizing I was in bed with Charlie. Only Charlie. And we were naked. I didn't give a shit if he saw my balls, or if he watched while I pleasured our woman, but that was as far as it went. If we were going to sleep without Grace, I had my own bedroom.

I climbed from the bed, grabbed my pants from the floor. I didn't bother with a shirt, only fastened one button so they'd stay on my hips. The sun was up, but by the angle, it was still early.

Hank rolled over. "Fuck, maybe she's making breakfast."

"We don't even know if she cooks," I countered. "I don't smell coffee, or bacon."

My stomach rumbled at the idea. We'd all worked up an appetite all night, taking her again and again. And the thought of what we'd done with her made my cock hard.

"Maybe she's at the creek washing up. From what she said yesterday, it didn't sound like she'd ever used a tub before. And, we got her pretty fucking dirty."

I grinned, shifted my cock in my pants. "How many times did we come in her?"

He sat up, then reached down and grabbed his pants. "Lost track."

His red hair was tousled from sleep and I could see scratches on his back from Grace's nails. Our wife was a wildcat.

I went downstairs, found the kitchen empty. The stove was cold. Looking out the back window, I didn't see her down by the creek.

I found the hastily scrawled note on the table as Charlie came into the room. I stared at it. Read it again. And again, trying to understand what I was seeing.

My smile slipped. My heart pounded. My happiness... gone. My cock stand... gone.

CARVER CITY BANK IS NEXT. *Noon today.*
I'm sorry.

"FUCK!" I shouted.

"What?" Charlie asked. I stuck my arm out and he grabbed the note from me. Read it. "I... I don't understand."

I crossed my arms over my chest. "She's one of them." My voice was as flat as the pancakes I'd hoped to have for breakfast.

"One of them?" He looked from the note to me. "You mean one of the Grove gang? No one ever mentioned a woman being among them."

I shrugged, paced the room. "She didn't dress like a woman until last night."

His eyes flared wide, then narrowed when he finally understood. Had Grace always been part of the gang who'd robbed and murdered, taken for a man?

"She shot two of her cohorts to get the money for herself. Maybe?" He ran a hand through his hair as he considered. "Fuck, she clearly had issues with men. She snarled and hissed like a feral cat until we petted that pussy."

"No one had been there before us," I stated, remembering how she'd responded the very first time by the creek.

"So she, what? Hates the Grove men enough to shoot them?"

"She didn't kill them, just left them for us," I reminded. "She didn't think we'd follow her, instead assumed we'd drag their sorry asses to jail."

"We definitely surprised her at that shanty. But we offered her the perfect scenario." His gaze met mine. Stated the plain truth. "Married to a fucking sheriff."

She was legally married to Charlie, but in Bridgewater, there was no difference. She was my wife, too, and I'd proved that to her all last night.

"An outlaw who marries a lawman." I shook my head, still stunned, still fucking pissed. I felt used. Cheated. *Robbed,* and not of money. Worse. "I said the vows, I fucked her. I took her virginity, felt that barrier break for my cock. My cum's still inside her, wherever the hell she is."

"Carver City, obviously," he snapped, waving the note in the air. "She's going to rob the bank."

"Why tell us then?" I wondered.

He shrugged. "It doesn't matter if she gets caught or not.

You're her husband. It's not like you're going to let her hang."

I wanted justice. I'd lived for nothing but since my father had been killed. She was one of them, one of the gang who shot him. Had she been the one to pull the trigger? She should hang. *Fuck!* I couldn't do it. There was no way I could see that happen.

I stormed outside, let the door slam against the house, set my hands on my hips. I took in the open prairie, the peace, completely at odds to how I felt inside.

"She not only stole from the bank, she stole my fucking dream," he said from behind me. "I wanted a wife, a family and she took that from me. Used it. Hell, she could be pregnant right now and what's going to happen? She'll hang along with Marcus and Travis Grove."

I never thought about a baby. After the night before, it was a strong possibility. Fuck. I turned to him. "I won't let that happen."

"What, keep her alive long enough to learn if she's with child? And if not, hang her?"

I dropped my head, stared at my bare feet. "I don't know. Fuck, I don't know. The only thing we do know about Grace right now is that she wants us to stop the bank robbery in Carver City. That's what we'll do."

And everything else, what we shared last night, how she responded, how she'd begged for more of our cocks... it was all a lie. Except her virginity. She hadn't faked that. Perhaps she'd saved that for just the right man. A man with a badge who could save her neck and a big cock to make her scream.

∽

GRACE

Sneaking out and leaving Charlie and Hank was the hardest thing I'd ever done. Last night had been perfect. Wild and untamed, gentle and cherishing. I'd felt special, the center of their world. Their everything. I'd given them *everything* in return.

And I would give even more to see them safe. They'd hate me. By now, they'd have found the note I'd left, know who I really was. Perhaps not my name, but that I was all wrong for them. That I was irredeemable.

I could live with that. It would hurt. It felt as if someone had shot me in the chest and I was able to survive even while slowly bleeding. But they would be safe. Whole. I wouldn't see them or any of my new friends at Bridgewater harmed.

Barton Finch wanted me to help him rob a bank. I'd do that. That didn't mean I'd help him get away. I wanted him behind bars like Father and Travis. I wanted him to face the judge for his crimes. I wanted him to hang for them. I'd see to it, even if it meant my demise as well. It was the only way I'd ensure those at Bridgewater would remain safe, that no other innocent people in the Territory would be robbed or terrorized or hurt. Or live and mourn after the death of an innocent loved one like Hank.

Barton Finch might rob a bank, but he was going to fucking jail.

∼

CHARLIE

. . .

I'D BEEN AN IDIOT. Falling for a woman on sight. And a woman dressed like a man. That should have been my first warning. But no. My cock wanted her. My head wanted her. My heart, well, it fucking wanted her. And now it was crushed. I felt like a pussy being so devastated by a mere woman. A mere woman I'd only known for two days.

Fuck.

But this wasn't a woman I bedded for the night, or even for the hour. I was no virgin, nor had I been a monk. From England to Mohamir to America, I'd had my fair share of pussy. Grace was different. Oh, she had the sweetest, tightest, most perfect pussy ever. But that wasn't it. I wanted more from her than just temporary pleasure.

I wanted forever. *Grace was mine.*

She had my ring on her finger. Hank's, too.

And we were hunting her down just as we had the Grove gang the other day. For being a fucking outlaw.

And yet, it was our job, our honor, to protect her. It was the way of those in Mohamir to cherish their wife. The reason for two men to claim a woman together was for her, to ensure she would be seen to if something happened to one of her men. The wife was the center of the family, the heart. Without someone guarding and watching out for her, it could be ruined.

It went against every bit of my personal honor to go after her like this. Robbing banks, even from the wrong side, was dangerous. She could be hurt, killed holding up the place, especially after the string of robberies. The tellers were on guard and nervous they would be next. Surely, they were armed and waiting.

We had to get to Grace before she got hurt. I'd protect her, then find out what the fuck was going on. She didn't need a noose about her neck, she needed a trip over my knee and a serious spanking. It had been beautiful to watch her give over to us, and she'd do it again, but this time, we'd have the truth. We wouldn't wait for it, we wouldn't assume we had the rest of our lives.

We'd asked her why she shot the Grove men. She'd said she'd been passing through and hadn't wanted to see us hurt. But where had she been and where had she been headed? Why hadn't she killed them? She could have, just tilting her gun slightly would have finished both men in an instant. Why the fuck did she wear pants?

So many questions unanswered. We should have asked them, but hadn't.

I spurred my horse to a faster gallop. I needed to know it all. I needed to know the truth.

∼

GRACE

I'D NEVER ROBBED a bank before. Even after living with Father and my brothers my whole life, I didn't even know how. That was why I was surprised Barton Finch wanted me along. His plan was to get in, get the money and get out. Get gone. He thought me a woman stuck under his control, that he could blackmail me into being his new partner in crime. I had to admit, he had plenty to hold over me.

Because I was a Grove, he considered me to be something I was not. I wasn't ruthless. I wasn't mean. I might have an infamous surname, but I was one no longer. The second I shot Father and Travis, I'd been done with them. I'd been ready to strike out on my own. Survive without them. Knowing they'd been caught and were no longer hurting people or wreaking havoc on the Montana Territory, I had been set free.

But then my heart had been caught in a snare so well hidden, I hadn't even known I'd been trapped. I'd been caught by love and that was something Barton Finch would never understand. His threat to kill those at Bridgewater, to hurt Charlie and Hank, was enough to bring me here, and I was willing to sacrifice myself so they could be safe.

What he didn't realize was that I wanted him gone. Wanted him caught. Captured. Hanged. Because if he'd tried to rape me, he'd surely done it to another woman in the past and would do it again. A man like him never changed.

I'd sacrifice myself for my husbands and newfound friends, but I'd take him down with me.

And so I'd played the role of exactly what he thought I was: a weak, simpleminded female.

I'd gone into the Carver City bank and stood there holding my gun and tried to look threatening. I was in my usual uniform of Travis' worn pants and shirt. I'd even found the binding for my breasts and wrapped them snuggly. My hair, back in the long braid, was tucked up under my hat. I didn't look much like a man, but I definitely didn't look like a lady.

Luckily, there were only the teller and the manager in the building when we entered. Carver City wasn't as big as the name implied. Most people in the area bartered or didn't have enough money to warrant a bank, instead stuck it in a coffee tin or beneath their mattress. But, there were some rich ranchers in the area, or those who needed loans.

Barton Finch entered the bank full of piss and vinegar,

shouting and waving his gun about to incite fear. I didn't point my weapon at anyone, but high up toward the ceiling. To Barton, who was at the counter and focused on the money the teller was shoving in a bag, I was doing my job. He'd told me I was to shoot anyone who entered or anyone who, as he'd said, even breathed funny. The only person I wanted to shoot was him and up until he waved the gun in the teller's face, he hadn't done anything wrong in the eyes of the law.

No one knew who he was or that he'd been part of the Grove gang. A third man was known and wanted, but not his name. If I'd shot him in cold blood, I'd have felt justice had been served. But then I'd have been the guilty one. A murderer. I had to ensure he was caught red-handed. And that was why we were standing in the bank robbing it.

A shot rang out. I jumped, startled out of my thoughts.

"I told you no weapons!" Barton Finch shouted, grabbing the gun the teller had pulled from beneath the counter. "Do it again and it'll be your head I aim for."

The teller had turned a ghastly shade of white and shoved the money into the bag with more haste, his entire body shaking.

Thank god he hadn't been shot.

The bag hadn't been closed or pushed across the counter when the entry doors burst open.

Hank and Charlie stormed in, guns raised, eyes sharp. Inwardly, I sighed and I tried not to smile at the sight of them. My heart flipped and knew they'd found my note. But when they glanced at me, all I saw was coldness. Hatred. My plan was working, but even though I'd known they'd hate me, it still hurt.

Barton Finch spun about, pointed his gun at the men.

"Don't even think it. Put the gun down," Hank ordered.

I'd never seen him like this. Focused and intent as usual, but he was driven by anger. He was handsome and virile, ruthless, and I loved him for risking his life for assholes like Barton Finch.

"Shoot him, Grace," Barton Finch snapped.

Hank kept his gaze on Barton Finch, but Charlie was watching me.

"What?" I asked, and began to shake, my weapon wavering. "I... can't."

"Why? Because he's your husband?" Barton Finch snapped. "Please, you're a Grove. Shoot the fucker."

Charlie's eyes flared wide and I saw the stiffening of Hank's shoulders.

Barton Finch noticed their reactions as well because he started to laugh. "You didn't know, Sheriff? You didn't know your own wife is an outlaw? You might have captured two of the Grove gang, but you missed one. Hell, you were between her thighs all night."

"You're Grace *Grove*?" Charlie asked.

I swallowed back the tears that threatened. Now wasn't the time to get upset. I had a plan and I had to follow it. I had to see it through, no matter the cost.

"You were part of all the robberies?" he wondered next.

"I... I..." I sputtered, then lowered my weapon.

"Her? Part of the robberies?" Barton Finch laughed.

Inwardly, I smiled. He did exactly as I'd expected. No woman could take credit for his efforts, no matter how dastardly.

"Look at her, she's too nervous to even wave a gun at you. I'm not," he snapped and cocked his weapon.

"No!" I shouted, lifting my gun and pointing it at Charlie and Hank.

Through all of this Hank remained silent. His eyes were on me now, narrowed, jaw clenched.

"Shoot them, Grace. I want to see you kill your own husband."

I swallowed, aimed my gun at Hank. Looked him in the eye. Fired.

12

Hank

Fuck. Holy fuck, she'd fired her weapon at me. I didn't think she'd do it, but it went to show how ruthless she was. How much she'd had us played all along. I'd married a fake. She was even worse than her father and brother. They hadn't hidden who or what they were. They wore their evil like a coat and that made Grace's duplicity even more wicked.

But then, I realized... she hadn't actually shot me.

She'd missed.

"He's fifteen feet in front of you! How could you *miss*?" The fucker shouted at her.

He was in his thirties, with scraggly hair, ragtag clothing. He looked like he hadn't seen water in a few months. But none of that mattered. It was the evil gleam in his eye.

He was filthy through to the bone.

When I looked at Grace, I didn't see that hardness. It wasn't something easily faked. What the fuck was going on here? There was no question this asshole was robbing the bank. There was no question Grace was robbing it with him. But she didn't seem to be *with* him.

If she really was Grace Grove, then she was taking her father's and brother's place in the gang. But why? Money? Why had she shot them in the first place the other day?

She had everything with us. Two men who loved her. Yes, love. A home. Friends at Bridgewater. Even a fucking copper tub.

Why did she leave it all for him? And why did she leave us a note to come here?

If she wanted to claim a rightful spot on the Grove gang, it didn't make sense to tell the sheriff where and when she was going to commit her next crime.

But it all came down to one thing. One bullet.

She hadn't shot me.

"I told you earlier, I'm a terrible shot," she said, pleading with the fucker. Who the hell was he anyway?

A terrible shot? Grace?

"You're a worthless bitch. Good for nothing but spreading your legs. But you're uppity and frigid. Worthless." He spit a wad of tobacco onto the bank's wood floor.

Grace wasn't a danger to us. She wasn't going to do us any harm. It was the man, the asshole who was talking shit about her, disrespecting her, who was my sole focus.

"That's my wife you're talking about," I growled.

He tipped his head back and laughed. "It must stick in your craw you've married a Grove. That you fucked a Grove. I've got the money, it's time to get gone," he said, the full satchel in one hand, waving his gun about with the other.

I knew what was coming. He wasn't letting us leave this bank alive.

"Clearly Grace is useless for shooting people. It's you or

me, Sheriff, and I think it's going to be you who's dying today."

Instead of being shot... again, a weapon fired. Again, it was Grace's. She'd spun lightning fast, when the fucker's attention had been on me and Charlie. His gun flew across the room as she'd shot his hand, right through the palm.

He screamed, clutched the wounded hand as he bent over. Blood dripped onto the floor. "You bitch! You shot me."

Grace walked over to him. Slow and easy. Her false fear was now gone. "The only person dying today, Barton Finch, is you."

"You set me up," he growled. Sweat dotted his brow, his skin becoming pale from pain.

"I'm just a worthless bitch, remember? How could I do something like that?"

"You're going to jail. You'll hang! Your own husband is going to put a fucking noose about your neck," the fucker she called Finch, snarled.

Grace smiled coldly. "Maybe, but I'll die knowing you're in hell while the men I love are safe. Just like my pa and Travis learned, no one fucks with my family."

Her voice was flat, even. Cold. I knew that look, the feeling coursing through her. Justice. Retribution.

Did she say love?

"You shot your own father and brother? They're your fucking family!" he shouted, grimacing in pain.

"No. They're not family. They didn't give a shit about me. Made me cook, clean. Beat me. *Gave* me to you as payment."

Fuck. I saw red then. If I didn't have a star pinned to my chest, and we weren't standing in a bank with witnesses, I'd have shot him through the head and left him for the coyotes to find. He wasn't worth digging a grave.

Finch actually grinned. "A man's dick doesn't get hard for anything in pants. I doubt you even have a pussy."

Grace raised her gun, pointed it at Finch's head, ready to do exactly what I wanted.

"Grace, no," I said and approached.

"He deserves to die," she countered, not looking away from the fucker.

"He does, and he will. But not by your hand."

She didn't need that in her mind. I knew what it felt like to kill, even a worthless piece of shit like Finch. It lingered. It wouldn't go away. Ever.

"Just like your father and brother. You shot them because of what they did to you, because they were going to kill us, but you didn't kill them."

"They'll be hanged?" she asked.

"No question."

"And him?" She didn't lower her weapon, still intent to finish him. I didn't care if Finch died, but I cared about how it would affect Grace.

"Absolutely."

"And me?" she asked.

I looked at her, back in those fucking pants and loose shirt. There was no sign of her curves and that meant she had that fucking strip of material wrapped over her gorgeous breasts. Her hat was tipped low over her face, but I couldn't remember how I'd ever thought her a man.

I knew how those lips felt on mine, on my skin. I knew what her pulse at her neck felt like against my lips. I knew the softness of her breasts, the feel of her tight nipple against the roof of my mouth. The taste of her pussy. The feel of it clenching my cock.

The way she looked when she came. I knew everything about her.

But then, I knew nothing about her at all.

"You'll pay for what you did."

GRACE

I HAD EXPECTED to be dragged back to Simms and jailed with Father, Travis and Barton Finch. To be locked up to await the judge and then sentenced to hang. Being with them until we were hanged would be far worse than dying. That would... I hoped, be swift.

If Charlie and Hank had seen me on the bluff, Father and Travis probably had as well, even writhing in pain. They'd know I was the one who shot them. Who'd left them to be arrested and put them in their current predicament.

Barton Finch would know I'd played him the fool.

Their necks were going to snap because of me and I wasn't sure if I would survive a jail cell in their company.

Barton Finch had his hands in cuffs upon one horse, Hank holding the reins with his gun out riding beside him. I'd been in Charlie's lap, his arms securely about my waist. As we rode into town, the more I worried, the more I panicked. Sweat dampened the binding about my breasts. My heart pounded as loud as a stampede and it was hard to catch my breath.

"Charlie, I'm sorry," I said for about the fiftieth time. I'd known what was coming. I'd known all along, accepted it. With Barton being yanked off his horse, swearing at Hank as he did so, I knew my plan had worked. Charlie and Hank were safe. Everyone at Bridgewater wouldn't be shot in their sleep. Still... I was scared.

He didn't respond this time, or any of the others. Gone was the quick smile, the easygoing nature. The gentleness.

Hank shoved Barton toward the jail and inside.

Charlie didn't move. Didn't force me down to follow.

"Charlie—"

"I don't want to hear it now, Grace."

His words were cold and smooth as ice on a winter pond. No *love* on the end.

Five minutes later, Hank returned, mounted his horse and we left town. Heading north, I knew instantly we were going to Bridgewater.

"I don't understand," I said, glancing from Hank and tipping my chin up to look at Charlie. He didn't look at me, just stared forward, his jaw clenched.

We rode straight to their house, the place I'd thought I'd never see again. Hank dismounted, then came over and helped me down. Charlie followed.

But we didn't go inside. Hank sat down on the steps that led to the front porch tugged me to stand between parted knees. Charlie settled beside him so I was eye to eye with both of them. One dark gaze, one green gaze boring into me as if they could see my soul.

There were times I thought they could, but Hank's next words made me realize they knew nothing.

"We're home. It's time to talk," Charlie said, reaching out and taking off my hat, just as they had by the creek when we'd first met.

My braid fell down my back.

Hank nodded his head in agreement. "I think it's time you introduce yourself, wife."

I swallowed, licked my dry lips. Had it only been dawn since I rode away from them?

"I'm... I'm Grace Grove." I sighed, relieved to finally say

it. To tell them the whole truth. "The name I used to marry you yesterday... Churchill, was my mother's maiden name."

"You shot your father and brother," Charlie said.

I nodded, my thumb rubbing over the material of my pants on my thigh. "Yes."

"Did you shoot my father?" Hank asked.

All the blood drained out of my face and little spots danced before my eyes. "Dear lord, no. It was Father. He got drunk, pleased with himself."

"Why?" Hank asked. "Why did you shoot your family?"

I sighed, flicked my gaze to his. There were no laugh lines at the corners of his eyes. There was no softness to him that I'd seen when we'd been in bed together. He'd shed his sheriff persona along with his clothing.

I didn't need the glint of sunlight off the badge on his chest to know who he was in this moment.

"Like I told you, they were going to shoot you. I couldn't let that happen."

"And?"

"And because I hate them and they deserved to go to jail."

"They beat you," Charlie said, clearly remembering what I'd said at the bank. I noticed his hands were clenched into fists.

"Father did when he was drunk. When he was mad."

"And Travis?"

I shook my head. "No, but he..." I looked down at the packed dirt at my feet.

"He what?"

"He didn't need to use his fists to hurt me. Our older brother, Tom, he wasn't as mean. He'd protected me from them. But then he'd was shot and killed. It got worse after that. And then the other day—"

I bit my lip, glanced away. I couldn't look at them, couldn't see either the pity in their eyes or the hatred.

"The other day?" Charlie prompted.

"Father had the bag with all the money from the Travis Point bank. That was the robbery before Simms. He spent most of it at the saloon. Poker. Women. When Barton Finch found out his portion had been used on pussy—"

Hank growled.

"That was his words, not mine," I clarified, putting a hand to my chest. "When he found out, he told Father he'd have to pay. So he gave me to Barton Finch as payment."

Both men went still, I glanced at them, and I didn't even think they were breathing.

"Gave you?" Hank finally whispered.

"To use as he wanted. I didn't know, but then he began to grope me, planned to rape me." I shivered, even in the bright sunshine. "I had no intention of allowing him what he wanted. I... I kneed him in the balls and got away. I was why Barton Finch didn't rob the Simms bank. He'd planned to be... busy with me." I clenched my fingers together, wrung them as I spoke. "I knew Father and Travis had robbed the bank and knew which way they'd go to return home. I came across you and, well, you know this part."

Hank cleared his throat.

"How many banks did you rob with them?"

My mouth fell open and surely flies could enter. "None!" I practically shouted. "I swear. I didn't do anything with them. They wouldn't let me since I was just a worthless woman. Not that I had aspirations to do so," I clarified, ensuring they knew I wouldn't have participated if they'd let me.

"And that fucker Finch?" Hank snapped.

"It was the three of them. Together. Except the Simms robbery."

"Then why would you join him today? Why rob with a man who intended to rape you? Money?"

I shook my head. Again and again. "He threatened me when Emma, Ann and I were in the mercantile. Threatened —" I bit my lip again.

Hank reached out, turned my chin back and held it with his fingers so I was forced to look at him. "Threatened who?"

"You." Tears welled in my eyes. Tears I'd not shed in years. My heart had been hardened; my life had been fucking hardened until I'd felt numb. Nothing. But now, these two men made me feel *everything.*

"He threatened me so you go off, by yourself, to rob a bank? To what, save me?" Hank snapped, tossed his hat down on the step beside him and ran his hand through his hair.

"He threatened both of you. I couldn't let him hurt you because of me. Don't you see? I'm a Grove. I'm... bad."

"And you married us so you could have protection. Obviously, we didn't put you in jail with the others," Hank said. His calmness had chipped away until his anger broke through.

"I married you because I wanted you. *Want* you." My words weren't enough to express what I felt.

Charlie held up his hand. "You married us *after* he threatened you. The perfect protection."

I shook my head. "I wanted one day of a real family. A real life. I knew I'd have to leave. Have to go with him otherwise he'd come to Bridgewater. Shoot you, shoot the others. Everyone would stay safe only if I went and did what he wanted. So I had the wedding I wanted, the wedding night I never expected. Two men I never dreamed would want *me*. Then I walked away."

They were quiet, but I saw Hank's eyes widen, his look change. "Oh fuck."

A hand came out, hooked about my waist and I was pulled into him. I felt his hardness, his heat. Breathed in his male scent.

"You sacrificed yourself. You expected to go to jail. To be hanged with them."

I looked away, but Hank's hand forced my head back. "I'm a Grove."

And with those words as the answer to everything that had happened, he leaned forward set his shoulder in my belly and stood so he was carrying me like a sack of potatoes.

He spun on his heel and carried me inside, up the stairs and into his room.

13

ANK

THE TRUTH WAS like a lightning strike. Sudden, severe and searing.

She stood before me and I grabbed both sides of her shirt, yanked. The buttons went flying across the room, fabric rented. I didn't give a fuck; she was never wearing that shirt again.

"You robbed a fucking bank to keep me and Charlie, as well as the others at Bridgewater safe. Planned to hang."

I glanced at Charlie, who, by the look on his face, had come to the same conclusions I had. He stood behind her, reached around and undid her pants. He dropped to his knees, got her out of them and her boots in seconds.

I grunted at the sight of the binding about her breasts. I found the little knot and loosened it, then tugged, forcing her to spin around in circles for it to unwrap. Charlie stood and moved out of the way.

"You not only told us where the robbery would be, but intentionally played a meek, flippant woman so Finch would get caught."

"All the while, you assumed you'd go to jail, too."

"I robbed a bank!" she said once the end of the binding was in my hand, the rest of it a coil on the floor. I let it drop, as if it were a snake. It would all be burned so she'd never be able to wear it again.

"You wore those stupid men's clothes!" I snapped. "I should spank your ass for that."

Her eyes widened to tea saucers. "You want to spank me for my clothing choice, not because I robbed a fucking bank?"

I grinned then. "There's my fierce Grace."

Hooking my hand behind her neck, I pulled her to me and kissed her. Fiercely. God, her taste, the heat of her, the softness of her lips. The aggressiveness of her tongue as it tangled with mine.

I finally let her up for air. "I don't understand," she murmured, her lips a bright pink and swollen. The rest of her was all pale skin, lush curves and other pink places. Places that made my mouth water to taste. My cock throbbed with the eagerness to fuck.

Charlie began to shuck his clothes. "You aren't Grace Grove. You're Grace Pine. My wife."

"And mine," I added.

"We're not going to spank you, we're going to fuck you," he said.

She tried to step back, but I wouldn't let her. Never again.

"Why?"

"Because you've got the sweetest pussy ever, love. I want you to know how much we want *you*. You're the center of our world, Grace. We're going to fuck you together, prove to you you're the one who makes us a family. Makes us whole," Charlie said earnestly. Fervently. Now naked, he stepped close to her, his front pressed to her back, and kissed her shoulder. "Because you told Finch you were protecting the men you love. *Love.*"

"You've never done anything wrong, sweetheart," I said. "Well, you should have told us from the beginning. It's our job to take on your problems. We're big men; we can handle the heavy weight."

Tears streamed down her cheeks, and I wiped them away with my thumbs.

"I was hell bent on justice. I got it. And you," I said. "We're not letting you go, sweetheart, even if I have to handcuff you to the bed."

Charlie raised his head and growled. "An excellent idea."

That made her laugh and Charlie smiled. The first time all fucking day.

"Are you ready to be ours, Grace Pine? Completely and with no secrets?" I wondered.

We were married yesterday, heard her say the vows, but now we knew the truth. Her answer now sealed her fate.

"Yes. Fuck, yes," she murmured.

Ah, that ladylike talk. I was content for the first time in… ever. Father would have fallen in love with Grace. All sass and fire, loyalty and devotion. Perhaps he'd sent her to us like I'd thought. I'd ended my quest for his killers and found a wife. The mother of our children.

Our world.

~

CHARLIE

. . .

I SPUN Grace about and kissed her. My hands roved over her, breasts and waist, ass and hips, finally settling over her pussy.

Drenched, just as I suspected. She might hide herself away, hide more than her emotions, but her body never lied. She wanted us. Needed us. And we'd give her everything her heart desired.

It would take a lifetime of effort trying to compete with what Grace had done for us. She'd expected to *die* to protect us. She'd gone off with the man who'd planned to rape her so we'd stay safe.

Yes, it was absolutely insane. We were men. Big men. Fuck, I'd been in the British military. I could protect Grace from that fucker. But she'd cared too much to see us hurt.

And so I would spend the rest of my life showing her how much we cared about her.

Starting right now.

My fingers slipped inside her and I brought her to a swift, ruthless orgasm. I had no intention of teasing her, to watch as she gave over to the pleasure. No, I wanted her to succumb to it like jumping off a cliff. No escape, nothing but the fall. Except we'd be there to catch her. Every time she jumped with us, we'd hold her. Keep her safe.

She would learn, by any means necessary, that we would always be there for her. When she screamed her pleasure, when her muscles went soft, her bones practically melted from pleasure, I scooped her up and placed her on the bed. Climbing over her, I kissed her, then worked my way down her body until I was between her thighs. Tossing her legs over my shoulders, I ate her pussy until she came again.

By then, she was a sweaty, begging bride eager for her husbands' cocks.

Hank had stripped down and dropped onto the bed beside her. I moved out of the way and he pulled her up and on top of him. "It's time, sweetheart."

She looked down at him, at his big cock.

"Up you go." With his hands on her hips, he lifted her up, then brought her back down. I watched his cock disappear inside her, saw the way her body took him deep. How she gasped and wiggled her hips to accommodate his large size.

I found the ointment Kane had given me before our wedding, the slick oil that would coat my cock and ease its passage into her virgin ass.

I watched as she rode Hank's cock, circling her hips and learning her pleasure in this position. I couldn't wait any longer and moved in to join them. With Hank's legs spread wide, I fit directly behind our bride, my cock sliding through the crack of her ass, brushing over the tiny hole I'd soon breach.

She was ours in every way. Our wife.

GRACE

I'D BEEN WRONG. So very wrong. They had no intention of sending me to jail. They did plan to send me to heaven. Charlie had brought me to climax twice and now I was close again riding Hank's cock. I had no idea we could fuck this way, but it was incredible. I loved how deep he went, how I could control how I moved. But then that thought fled my mind like a cloth erasing words on a chalk board.

Charlie's cock pressed against my back entrance and I stilled, looked over my shoulder.

"Deep breath, love. I'm going to take you, too. This hole we played with is going to open for my cock."

He pressed against me as Hank remained still. His hands, which had been on my hips, slid over my belly, then higher to cup my breasts.

"Come kiss me," he murmured, and I leaned forward.

Our tongues tangled as Charlie continued to press and retreat, then press some more.

I gasped when I opened for him all at once, the broad head of his cock popping inside me. "Charlie!" I groaned.

His hand settled on my shoulder and I could hear his ragged breathing. "Bloody hell, love. You're so tight."

"I'm not going to last," Hank said. Sweat dotted his brow and he looked strained, as if holding himself still was the worst kind of torture.

I panted as Charlie worked his way further into me, little in and out motions that were eased by something slick.

"There," he breathed.

"I'm so... oh, god I'm so full."

I was. With both of them.

"That's right, love. You're so full of us. Our cocks, all of us. You've got every bit of us."

"Including our hearts," Hank added. "Now move."

Charlie laughed behind me and began to pull back. Hank thrust his hips up.

My breath caught and I held onto Hank's shoulders as if I could keep myself from going anywhere. I wasn't. I was pinned between them, taking them, feeling them. Getting everything from them.

They fucked me in alternating motions. In. Out. Slow and smooth until I couldn't take it anymore. They were overpowering, in all ways.

"Charlie!" I cried. "Hank!"

I came then, squeezing and clenching on their cocks, holding them in, taking them deeper.

They gave me everything and I took. Yet I gave them everything as well.

We were one. I felt them come, the hot spurts of their seed deep inside me.

Charlie carefully pulled out, then Hank and I was tucked between them. Their hands continued to roam, their lips kissing my sweaty skin.

"You're our prisoner, love," Charlie whispered as I was sinking into sleep.

"That's right, sweetheart. The sentence is life."

Just as I wanted it.

NOTE FROM VANESSA

Guess what? I've got some bonus content for you with Grace, Hank and Charlie. So sign up for my mailing list. There will be special bonus content for books, just for my subscribers. Signing up will let you hear about my next release as soon as it is out, too (and you get a free book...wow!)

As always...thanks for loving my books and the wild ride!

EXCERPT FROM ROSE

A historical romance in the Wildflower Brides series with a feisty heroine and an alpha cowboy determined to make her his.

Rose Lenox has always been more comfortable on the back of a horse than wearing ribbons and bows. For years, she's been content working on the family ranch, but lately she's finding herself wanting more. She's determined to strike out on her own and find freedom from her unorthodox family.

Chance Goodman has watched Rose grow up from a spitfire little girl into a fiery woman. He's wanted her for years, waiting patiently until he could make her his. When she leaves the Lenox ranch determined to abandon her former life and to stay good-bye to him, he knows now is the time he must claim her. Letting her go isn't an option.

Read Rose now!

ROSE - CHAPTER 1

ROSE

The kitchen at six in the morning was akin to what I remembered of busy Chicago intersections—crowded, loud and slightly dangerous. With ten women in the house, there was never quiet, never any peace. It was the same, day in and day out. Dahlia bickered with Miss Esther about how the bacon should be cooked. Poppy stood behind Lily and styled her blond hair in another inventive creation. Marigold set the table with a loud clatter of dishes, eager for her meal. Hyacinth sat at the large table humming placidly to herself as she sewed on a button. Iris and Daisy were most likely still asleep or at least taking their time in dressing as to avoid morning chores. I paused and watched the hubbub, shaking my head at the claustrophobic feel in the room.

Nothing had changed. The room had not changed since the first day we'd all arrived from Chicago sixteen years before. Besides being older, *no one* had changed; our personalities were as varied as ever. Except me. *I'd* changed. Why did everyone irk me? Why did the house suddenly seem so small? Why did my sisters seem so grating? Why did I feel like I was being suffocated?

Wanting to escape, I dropped the armful of wood into the bin beside the stove and walked right back outside, and started across the grass to the stable. I took deep breaths of the cool morning air in an attempt to settle myself. It was too early to be riled, especially from just the normal morning routine.

"Rose!" Miss Trudy's voice carried all the way to me. There was more than physical distance between us; there was an emotional separation as well. I stopped and turned back with a sigh, tucking my unruly hair behind my ear. The woman who'd raised eight orphan girls, myself included, held up a folded cloth. "If you won't eat at the table, at least take something with you."

Her hair was up in a simple bun at her nape of her neck, the gray in her red hair bright in the sun just breaking over the mountains. She was still beautiful, even with the fine lines that showed her age. As I mounted the steps to take the food, I saw concern in her green eyes, but refused to speak of it.

I smelled the biscuits and bacon and my stomach rumbled. "Thanks," I replied, with a semblance of a smile on my lips.

"Where will you be?" she asked, her voice calm and placid. She never shouted, never raised her voice.

No one went off without sharing their whereabouts, for dangers abounded the ranch and all of Montana Territory beyond.

"I'll follow the fence line to look for any sections that might need repair." There was no damaged fence line. I

Rose - Chapter 1

knew it and so did Miss Trudy, but she only gave a small nod, allowing me to escape.

Not sure what else to say, I turned to head towards the stable. I couldn't tell her I was unhappy, although I was sure she knew. Uttering the words would make me seem ungrateful. She and Miss Esther had provided a stable, loving home for all of us girls. I would have grown up in a large city, never knowing the open expanses and big sky of Montana if they hadn't claimed us all and brought us west. The thought had me rubbing the space above my heart, guilt and a restlessness pressing heavily. No matter the depth of her caring or the closeness I had with the other girls, I needed more. I needed to escape.

"Whatever that fence post did to you, it sure is sorry now."

The deep voice that came from behind me was such a surprise that I hit my thumb with the hammer. I was a mile from the house when I'd decided to work out some of my frustrations on the fence. The post had had a loose nail and I'd begun to pound it in, continuing to strike even after it was lodged back in the wood. I was still hammering when he caught me unawares.

I sucked in a breath at the searing pain in the tip of my thumb, holding the base of it in my other hand. I let a few less-than-ladylike words slip out as I winced, walking around in a circle.

"Chance Goodman!" I shouted, my anger and pain loud and clear. "You don't sneak up on someone like that."

The man was ten years older than I and lived on the nearest ranch. His parents had died a few years earlier and with much success, he'd taken over the spread, adding more cattle and even studding out his prized bulls. The latter made me flush every time I thought of it, for I knew what happened between a man and a woman—Miss Trudy and Miss Esther were former brothel owners and had given each of us girls a special talk—and I'd always pictured Chance's face in my mind when I imagined such acts. I'd seen one of his bulls and the...the thing that hung down from beneath its belly and it had me wondering what Chance would look like. Would he be large himself? Would he be just as aggressive when he mounted a woman? My nipples always tightened into hard points and I felt slickness between my legs every time I imagined such a scenario.

There was no other man for fifty miles who was so fine a specimen of manhood as Chance Goodman. I'd thought so when I was nine, and I thought the same now at nineteen. His hair was a chocolate brown which he let run toward the overly long. He towered over me; I only came up to his shoulder and made me feel...feminine. There were eight women in the house who cared about ribbons and lace when I was more interested in saddle leather and branding. But Chance often made me wish I'd combed my hair or worn clothing that made me appear more comely, at least in his eyes.

It wasn't his broad shoulders or thickly corded forearms that had my heart pounding whenever I saw him. It wasn't the way a dimple dented his cheek whenever he smiled. It wasn't the strong jaw nor the big hands so much as his dark eyes that attracted me. He was the only person who passed whatever facade I raised to hide my true self. It was as if I were constantly exposed, every emotion and feeling I had was clear as spring water to him. I couldn't hide from him, even when, like now, he stood right before me.

"Here, let me see." He took my hand as I turned toward

him. Before I could step away, he lifted it up so he could look at it, then, to my complete and utter surprise, slipped my injured thumb into his mouth. My own mouth fell open in utter surprise. My thumb was in Chance Goodman's mouth...and it felt good. His tongue flicked over the injured tip, sucking on it as if withdrawing the pain as he would venom from a snakebite. His mouth was hot and wet and my finger pulsed—among other places—and it wasn't from the hammer.

"What...what are you doing?" I asked, my words tumbling out in a confused rush. Chance had never even touched me before. He'd given me his linked palms to use as a step to mount a horse, but that was nothing compared to this. The way his dark eyes captured mine as his tongue flicked over my thumb was new. Gentle, possessive, *hot*. God, this was the most carnal thing I'd ever experienced and it was just my thumb! What would happen to me if he took even greater liberties?

At that enticing and very scary thought, I tugged my hand back. He could easily have kept it, for his strength was so much greater than mine, but he released me of his own choosing.

"Better?" he asked. His voice was deep and rough, reminding me of stones in the river.

I could only nod in response, as I was still flustered.

"I think this is the first time I've made you speechless." The corner of his mouth turned up and his dimple appeared.

I put my hands on my hips, ignoring the pain. "What do you want?" I asked, my tone acerbic.

His gaze raked over my body, assessing. He sighed. "Right now? I want to know what's wrong."

"Besides my thumb?" I held my hand up. "Nothing," I

grumbled.

"Rose," he said, his voice raised in that irritating warning tone.

"What? Can't a girl have some secrets?"

His dark eyebrows went up. "Since when do you consider yourself a girl?" He glanced down at the pants I wore instead of the skirt or dress of every other female. The barb stung, for it only validated my earlier insecurities. He didn't think of me as a woman. He thought of me as...Rose. Plain Rose in pants. What man could ever be interested in a woman who'd rather wear pants than ribbons and lace? What man could desire a woman who hammered fence posts?

"Since...." I clamped my mouth shut. "Oh, bother." I turned away from him and stomped off.

"Is Dahlia pestering you again?" he called out. "Or did Marigold eat your breakfast?"

I knew he was toying with me, for he'd never poke fun at the other girls. He was too much of a gentleman. It didn't keep him from poking fun at *me*. When Miss Trudy and Miss Esther found us girls, orphaned after the great Chicago fire, they hadn't known our names. Why they gave us all names of flowers, I'll never know. Moving to the Montana Territory had been a way for all of us to start over, especially Miss Trudy and Miss Esther. Well off from their years running a big city brothel, they'd wanted a new life and found it outside the town of Clayton. We were infamously known as the Montana wildflowers and were always considered as a group of eight, not as individuals.

"Everyone is the same. *Nothing's* changed."

"Are you wanting something different then?" He leaned a hip against the battered fence post, relaxed and at ease with himself while offering me his complete attention. I saw his horse in the distance, head lowered and nibbling grass. A bird flew overhead, its wings still as it rode a wind current.

"Something different? Of course I want something different!" I waved my arms in the air as I spoke. "I want to be independent, wild. Free! Not stuck in a house full of women who gab all day long about hairstyles and dress sleeve length. I want to do what Miss Trudy did—strike out and discover a whole new life in a far off land."

He patiently let me vent my spleen. "What do you plan to do?"

"I don't know, Chance, but I'm about to burst out of my own skin. Don't you see? I don't belong here anymore." I lowered my head with that admission, for I felt shame and guilt press heavily on my heart. Miss Trudy and Miss Esther had done so much for me, for all of the girls, and I was tossing all those years, all the love aside. I pressed once again to that spot on my chest as I felt tears well. Lifting my head to the sky, I sniffed and forced the tears back. I didn't cry. I *never* cried and I was mad at Chance for making me feel this way.

With his long stride, he walked toward me through the tall grass and tilted my chin up with his fingers, forcing me to look at him. My hat fell off my head to dangle by the long cord around my neck. His scent, a mixture of warm skin and pine and leather was something I associated solely with him. "No. You don't belong here anymore."

I couldn't believe that he agreed with me. The one person who I expected to fight for me—my friend—agreed with me. He wanted me to leave. I tore my chin from his hold and stomped over to my horse, quickly mounting. Using the reins to turn the animal, I gave Chance Goodman one last look. It was time to move on; he'd just confirmed that for me. My heart hurt, knowing I'd never see him again.

I settled my hat back on my head, gave it a little flick with my finger in farewell and rode off. Not only did the tip of my thumb ache, but also my heart.

Read <u>Rose</u> now!

GET A FREE BOOK!

Join my mailing list to be the first to know of new releases, free books, special prices and other author giveaways.

http://freeromanceread.com

ALSO BY VANESSA VALE

Grade-A Beefcakes

Sir Loin Of Beef

T-Bone

Tri-Tip

Porterhouse

Skirt Steak

Small Town Romance

Montana Fire

Montana Ice

Montana Heat

Montana Wild

Montana Mine

Steele Ranch

Spurred

Wrangled

Tangled

Hitched

Lassoed

Bridgewater County Series

Ride Me Dirty

Claim Me Hard

Take Me Fast

Hold Me Close

Make Me Yours

Kiss Me Crazy

Mail Order Bride of Slate Springs Series

A Wanton Woman

A Wild Woman

A Wicked Woman

Bridgewater Ménage Series

Their Runaway Bride

Their Kidnapped Bride

Their Wayward Bride

Their Captivated Bride

Their Treasured Bride

Their Christmas Bride

Their Reluctant Bride

Their Stolen Bride

Their Brazen Bride

Their Rebellious Bride

Their Reckless Bride

Their Bridgewater Brides- Books 1-3 Boxed Set

Outlaw Brides Series

Flirting With The Law

MMA Fighter Romance Series

Fight For Her

Wildflower Bride Series

Rose

Hyacinth

Dahlia

Daisy

Lily

Montana Men Series

The Lawman

The Cowboy

The Outlaw

Standalone Reads

Twice As Delicious

Western Widows

Sweet Justice

Mine To Take

Relentless

Sleepless Night

Man Candy - A Coloring Book

ABOUT THE AUTHOR

Vanessa Vale is the *USA Today* Bestselling author of over 60 books, sexy romance novels, including her popular Bridgewater historical romance series and hot contemporary romances featuring unapologetic bad boys who don't just fall in love, they fall hard. When she's not writing, Vanessa savors the insanity of raising two boys and figuring out how many meals she can make with a pressure cooker. While she's not as skilled at social media as her kids, she loves to interact with readers.

www.vanessavaleauthor.com

Manufactured by Amazon.ca
Bolton, ON